I FEEL LIKE
THE MORNING STAR

I FEEL LIKE
THE MORNING STAR

Gregory Maguire

1817

HARPER & ROW, PUBLISHERS
Cambridge, Philadelphia, St. Louis, San Francisco, London,
Singapore, Sydney, Tokyo
NEW YORK

I Feel Like the Morning Star
Copyright © 1989 by Gregory Maguire
All rights reserved. No part of this book may be used or reproduced in any manner whatsoever without written permission except in the case of brief quotations embodied in critical articles and reviews. Printed in the United States of America. For information address Harper & Row Junior Books, 10 East 53rd Street, New York, N.Y. 10022. Published simultaneously in Canada by Fitzhenry & Whiteside Limited, Toronto.
Typography by Joyce Hopkins
1 2 3 4 5 6 7 8 9 10
First Edition

Library of Congress Cataloging-in-Publication Data
Maguire, Gregory.
  I feel like the Morning Star / by Gregory Maguire.
    p.   cm.
  Summary: Three teenagers in a post-holocaust survival colony find that their shelter has become a prison and decide to break out.
  ISBN 0-06-024021-0 : $ ISBN 0-06-24022-9 (lib. bdg.) : $
  [1. Nuclear warfare—Fiction.   2. Survival—Fiction.] I. Title.
PZ7.M2762Iaf 1989   88-21544
[Fic]—dc19   CIP
                                                                AC

This book is for Mark Miller,
who is a lasting surprise.

Table of Contents

This is the shape of the leaf, and this of the flower,
And this the pale bole of the tree
Which watches its bough in a pool of unwavering
    water
In a land we never shall see.

—Conrad Aiken
"Priapus & the Pool, IV"

PART ONE

Something odd was sitting on a folding chair in the middle of the room. It was furred with its own body light, velveted in a brassy broth of shining. It was running its indistinct fingers through the layered thatch of its enormous wings, flicking out bits of dust. Its skin was shell pink, peach, sap golden, moon white. Its face and most of its naked limbs were hidden in the luminous fan of its blood-orange feathers.

The other folks didn't seem to see it. And as it tidily patted the scalloped edges of its wings into place, it ignored them, too.

The others were gossiping about prisons. Leper colonies, penal colonies, space colonies. The Annex, the Ghetto, Devil's Island.

They're all the same, someone was saying.

Stone walls do not a prison make, someone else was chanting softly.

3

He left the safety of the shadows and walked up behind the thing in the chair. He touched its shoulder blade, just where the left wing met the back in a complicated joint. His hand turned cream colored, grew warm. The thing stood, in a movement like a cat stretching after a nap, and the folding chair melted away.

Take me, he said to it. The others won't mind.

The thing never turned its head. But it must have heard him. It rotated both its wings backward to fold over him from collarbone to calf, like a feathery papoose. He leaned forward into the burnished hollow of its back, feeling the glow of hope steal over him, win him like a prize. A touching of dry aromatic moss against his closed eyelids, his lips, his chest . . .

Alcatraz, Sing-Sing, Elba, they were saying. Siberia, Auschwitz, Dachau.

The impossible was happening. He was escaping. This winged agent was his guide, his rescuer. His ticket to freedom. His emigration officer. His guardian angel. He threw his arms around its lovely neck.

The floor was falling back, the people dwindling. The thing rose in the air, against gravity and toward the ceiling. No one noticed. Then it flexed its mighty bedspread wings to take him out, across the border of metal ceilings and all else, and he slipped from his place, and dropped heavily, back through the litany of prisons to the torture of the floor.

1/ Waking

The first thing he knew was that his heart was slamming away inside him like a finch caught in someone's hands. It bashed with such ferocity that he almost shouted. He tried to shout. His voice was just a thread in his throat, attached to nothing, tugging at nothing—no sound came out.

He was waking up with a fright. He had twitched himself awake, or shivered, or something. There was nothing different about this fright. Good old dependable fright. It could be managed. It could be handled. Dr. Worth had told him how.

Ask yourself who you are. Ask yourself where you are. Establish yourself in the waking world—that's the first step to lowering your pulse, stilling the pounding in your ears.

He lifted himself up on one elbow in the thorough dark. Pillow and sheets were wet—he'd been dribbling and spewing again. He dabbed at the damp spots with the sleeves of his night tunic.

What is your name?

Sorb.

Where are you now?

Flat out in the flat characterless dark. Lying on a bed. Racked up in a metal bed just like the four hundred other people in this colony. Slapped down on a metal bed in this dense dark metal world. Tucked inside a steel skin. Bolted in place by the pitch black.

Why are you leaning on one elbow in the blackness, grinding your teeth out of kilter, perspiring as if you've just completed a fifty-yard dash?

Because of—because of—

He sat up intently, struggling with the void in his mind. Backtrack. Don't give up.

Who are you?

Sorb.

Where are you?

The Pioneer Colony.

How old are you?

Fifteen years old.

Where is your family?

My family is—my family is—gone. I am my only family.

Where are your friends?

Here. Near here. In the Colony.

Who are your friends?

Faces came to mind, but names? What were their names? The faces were beating like embers in a dying fire, steady and warm, and *bright*, so there must be names to go along.

Ella. And Mart. Ella and Mart.

Ella: full of sassy grace. Dark skin, the color of roasted almonds, and close-cropped curly hair—black, almost metallic blue. Ella bending at the waist, a curtsy to him, smile as contagious as the pox.

Mart: narrow and sharp, all ribs and serrations. Jagged blond hair, eyes with a purpose, and a heart like an ancient army tank.

With those two in mind—good old Ella, good old Mart—Sorb was suddenly and clearly awake. He fell backward, exhausted. So here you are, and you are only Sorb. How do you rate, having these dramatic anxieties? You're only Sorb. A natural-born dreamer. How does the heart see itself? Funny dark-haired Sorb, quirky-looking, lopsided, all those Asian and Mediterranean genes still skittering around inside, surprised at each other. Soft brown skin, no adolescent stubble to shave yet (the luck of the Filipinos, Mom used to boast). Heavy eyebrows from the Greek side of the family. Funny Sorb.

Normal as dishwater. Kind. Lazy. Elastic limbs, double-jointed. Temperament of a goldfish: complacent. But fond of a lark, of making people laugh, tying them together in a joke, a discussion.

Always trying to remake his family. Reinvent it.

A natural-born dreamer.

He'd been dreaming. And that was why he'd woken in a sour sweat.

But dreams, dear Lord, were nearly a punishable offense.

He closed his eyes. The dark inside him was no fiercer than the dark outside. Inside his private dark he tried to remember his dream, but the wraith lingered out of reach. He rolled, twisted his sheets, arched his feet several times to work out kinks in his muscles. Just before he fell asleep again, he realized that his mouth was worked into a strange grin even as his eyes were saltily filling and leaking, again, again.

2/ Pioneer Colony

When Sorb awoke, for real, with a full bladder and the quiet sense of dread that suffused every morning, he knew that his dream had been more powerful than any other he'd had in the past five years. Usually he remembered his dreams in shreds, a dim sense of places visited and people contacted, but no firm recollection of *where* and *who*. But for Sorb, the *where* and the *who* of his dreams, however strange and fantastic, were growing realer by every passing night.

He sat up in bed. Slowly he tried to reconstruct his dream. The feel of those angel's wings around him. The hope of escape. It seemed so possible, so real, that the molded plastic wall of his cubicle appeared odd and *unreal*. He reached out to touch it, trying to recall the confines of the Pioneer Colony. It was as if dream was boiling up inside him, soft, steamy, pervasive, slowly eating away at his sense of what was actual, the *here* and the *now*.

So he got up and left his cubicle, and wandered out of his compound, and made his way to the public access terminal. More than once before he'd felt the need to do this, early in the morning. It was becoming a dangerous kind of habit. Because he was breaking curfew there was no one around to see him, fortunately. He wouldn't want to have to admit that many mornings he couldn't quite remember where he was.

He called up the entry on the Pioneer Colony. *This is where you are,* he said to himself. *Keep it in mind.* On the purplish glare-resistant screen the encyclopedia description of his home came rolling up for him to read.

The Pioneer Colony.

Located in the Pioneer Valley north of Springfield District (in the State of Massachusetts by traditional nomenclature), the Pioneer Colony is the prototype and preeminent example of closed-access survival communities in the United States. Built to house a core community of one thousand members, with facilities to increase to one thousand four hundred, the Pioneer Colony utilizes the most advanced technologies to provide for regular and renewable resources required for basic human survival: air, water, nutrients, minerals, medicines.

The Pioneer Colony is situated some four thousand feet below the surface of the earth. Its closed-access status virtually insures for its inhabitants 100% survivability potential from attack by any currently cataloged nuclear or chemical weapon.

A complex system of lottery selections has been set in place; it is corrected to account for fair distribution of inhabitants regarding age, sex, and racial origin. In the event of a national catastrophe, the Federal Emergency Selection Service (FESS) will cull individuals for temporary housing and survival in the Pioneer Colony. It is anticipated that tenure in the Pioneer Colony will not exceed two years, although indefinite residence is possible. When funding is approved, FESS intends to replicate the model of Pioneer Colony outside several hundred urbs.

For diagrams, scroll to Appendix 153-Y.

Sorb scrolled away. He ought to know the entry by heart, he'd read it so often, but even now it made his mouth taste bitter as if he'd belched up some sour, acidic bile. Two years, hah. It was already four years and then some. And so much for "fair distribution of inhabitants"; Sorb was there simply because—because—

He didn't want to think about it. He leaned down and studied the plans.

He knew them so well, but to look at them again was to remember once more that he and the other four hundred inhabitants were, quite simply, buried alive in a tomb. A massive: spheroid: steel-reinforced-concrete: tomb. Here they were, the walking dead. Too well-behaved to lay down and die.

The Colony was a series of three concentric globes. The smallest and innermost was called the Centrex. It housed the rings of apartments—called compounds—which were arranged in three levels around the central gallery. The gallery was the heart of the Centrex and the Colony both, and, Sorb thought with some disdain, as hollow as a drum.

The second globe, or Utility Belt, ran like a skin around the Centrex. Filled with offices, labor sta-

11

tions, mechanical and technical apparatus, it was the working layer of the Colony—its nervous system, its creaky bowels and dried-out glands.

Around this, larger still, was the third globe, known as the Reaches. Sorb named it the Out-of-Reaches: a series of computer-generated locks and warning devices limited the access to approved personnel only. The gates were called drylocks because they kept the interior of the Colony dry and free of contamination from the musty storage areas of the Reaches. From there, if Sorb remembered correctly, ran the three collapsed tunnels to the World at Large.

If there was a World at Large.

He found himself pointing to the screen, locating himself in the tiny cubicle marked Public Access Terminal/Library. Snug in a grid-screened map of a tight-fisted world. That was the *here* and the *now* for Sorb. He mustn't forget it. This was the *where* and he was the *who*. There were no angels, there was no escape. This was it.

He flipped off the terminal, remembering that it was Ella's birthday today. He'd made plans to meet her and Mart at dawn, give her a birthday present. She was more real than any angel; she was part of the *who* and *where* of his life. But at the unconvinced edge of his mind nagged the stubborn suggestion that *who* and *where* weren't enough for him. There was still the impatient and unsatisfied *why?*

And he didn't know why.

3/ Morning

Nothing put Mart in a better mood than the thought of breaking a law or two. And the more inventive the crime, the better.

He snapped his fingers in rhythm, one two three four. He tapped a beat on the wall as he walked. He didn't see himself as a vessel of high spirits, usually, but today was special. He'd slapped a little of the flowery stinkwater on his cheeks and neck to make himself smell pretty; he'd even clipped his stupid nails. He felt like a sharpshooter in the old films, cautious and careless at the same time, clicking his shiny spurs down the main street of town. A sharpshooter on the wrong side of justice, of course.

The spotless corridors of molded plastic walls and ceilings, steel floors and recessed lights, didn't do very well at playing the part of a dusty main street in Cheyenne or Laramie. No barroom doors or boardwalks, just remote-controlled, eight-paneled door hatches and ramps. No tender breath of a western sunrise, distant rooster blurting out for its breakfast—just the mechanical hum as all the lights across the Colony kicked on, and morning, in a fraction of a second, once again took over from night.

He pushed open the door to the amity room. Ella and Sorb were already there, rubbing their eyes in the sudden dawn. Good, they'd broken curfew successfully too. Ella looked like heaven, and Sorb like something gone through the meat press.

"Good morning, Mart, we've been here fifteen minutes. I fell asleep again," said Ella, wriggling herself to a sitting position. "I thought you were the j-guards finding us out, the way you burst in with the light coming on just like that."

Mart swung into the small room and knocked against them meanly, kindly. In such a dingy, common, tiny cell, he felt wily and awake, as unruly as carbonation surging in a capped bottle. "Morning," he said. "Sorb, you look rotten. Another bad night?"

"So-so," said Sorb, pulling himself up. "At least it's morning."

"Morning, it's a dead word, there are no real mornings here," said Mart, cracking his knuckles.

"Oh, Mart," said Ella, "it's a *good morning*, okay, because we all got up before curfew-lifting, and we sneaked out without being caught by the j-guards, all three of us. And it's my birthday. So can we leave it at that? Or did you forget?"

"You know I didn't," he said. "But I'm not just being cranky. Look at us here. Three kids in a steel cradle—"

14

"I am sixteen today, I am a *woman!*" She made a sultry growl.

"Okay, okay, two fifteen-year-old boys and a tiger lady, all right?—and here we are. You climb up on the bench there and look out. Go on. Tell me what you see."

"Mart, cut it out. Don't be the big boss." Ella let out an editorial yawn.

He was feeling dramatic. He bounded onto the plastic bench himself and pointed out the window. "Do you see a sunrise? Do you see a golden dawn? Do you hear birds yapping it up among themselves? No. You see the gallery—a three-story well made of vomit-colored rubber"— he started laughing at himself— "at the bottom of which are our dearly beloved companions, trudging around saying good morning to each other. We've got regulation light, processed air, three meals a day, and a heart-attack system of bells. One day is different from the next? Morning is different from night?" He glared at them with mock ferocity. "Care to *argue* with *me?*"

Sorb was still looking sick. Ella was mouthing the words *ho hum* at him. He jumped down.

"So we *say* it's morning," said Mart, "but we three kids are barely old enough to remember what morning is supposed to be like. So it's another dead word and we shouldn't use it. Case closed. Happy birthday."

They sat down on the floor. The amity rooms weren't made for three, so they had to sit appetizingly close. Sorb apologized for jostling, and Mart said that *jostling* in the Pioneer Colony must be a dead word,

15

too—foreplay was better. Ella smacked him for being fresh.

"It's my birthday. Treat me with respect," she said. She was in uncommon good spirits too, Mart realized. She'd be ripe for his suggestion, as long as he could get rid of Sorb. If only Sorb didn't look so bedraggled again. What a case Sorb was: either the life of the party or—the death of the party. No middle ground for Sorb.

"Time's a-rollin' on, morning or not," said Mart sharply, feeling a twinge of guilt at conniving to sneak away without Sorb. "Come on, let's get this over with."

Sorb shifted around and drew from inside his tunic a small package wrapped in old news sheets. "This is it, our happy birthday from both of us," he said. "You have to help sing, Ella, even though it's your own birthday. You know we can't sing."

They began to warble it out, the happy birthday song, and Ella obeyed their vigorous gestures and joined in. Then she pulled the elastic bands off the package, and the paper fell away in curls. "What is it? I can't imagine—*ohhhhhh.*"

She held it up, as if they'd never seen it before. It was Sorb's precious salmon-colored seashell from the coast of East Africa, suspended on a delicate chain that went through a small hole in the shell. "There's nothing like it!" she said and, holding it carefully, kissed Sorb on the cheek, and then Mart. "What do you hear when you listen to the shell? The sea?"

"Not the sea," said Sorb, as they all rose to leave.

"Sea music, I think. Like—Handel's *Water Music*. From that old tape, I remember the part that goes: da, da, dadadada dum dum dadada—"

"Oh, don't," she said, and rushed her hands to her ears, but Mart could see that it was too late. The memory of the music had struck her, and she was angry and defenseless in the face of it. "You mean the Hornpipe in F," she said. "It'd be a pretty important seashell to broadcast stuff like that."

They stood in the doorway, watching her. She had on a sorry look. "My fault, whoops," said Sorb. "Sing it, get it out of your system. We'll wait."

"I can't sing," she said miserably. But she raised her right hand as if she were holding a baton, gave the upbeat, and came in with what murmuring noise she could permit from her own throat. More the tongue against the back of the teeth than anything else. Her hands arabesqued in six-eight time. Her eyes closed. Her eyelids looked soft, translucent, like the gloss on the inside of the seashell. Mart could stare at her for an hour when she looked like that.

The time alarm, buzzing its unmusical blat, interrupted her. "Come on, we'll be late for breakfast," said Sorb, "and you know how Mem Lotus loves to sing her 'Happy Birthday'!" He veered on his heel and started off.

Mart thought: now.

He grabbed her arm and said softly, "Wait!"

"Why?" she whispered.

"Just do it—make some excuse—"

"Sorb," she called, with astounding normalcy in her

17

voice, "you go on ahead. Say I'm feeling sick. I *am* feeling sick, I think. I think I'll go to the infirmary."

Sorb turned, already ten steps away, and arched his eyebrows quizzically. "Are you sick?" he said. Mart glanced away, guessing at a look of hurt on Sorb's face and not wanting to see it.

"Yes," said Ella, too quickly.

"Oh," said Sorb. "Well, okay." The voice didn't sound so bad. Mart stole a look against his better judgment, and then was sorry he had. Sorb's eyebrows had fallen, his jaw was set again, there were shutters in his face behind his dark eyes. "See you in class," said Sorb evenly, "if you make it."

A few minutes later, when Sorb had gone and they were tired of standing alone feeling bad about what they'd just done, Mart said, "Well, come on, pardner, we gotta make tracks."

"*Are* we going to make it to class?" said Ella. "Where are we going?"

4/ Breaking Out

He had to keep himself from grinning. "Someplace you've never been before. Just keep quiet and stay close."

"You're not going to do something stupid. Mart?"

"Not stupid. Special. This is an extra birthday present. In fact, since C-Day is the day after tomorrow, you can call this a C-Day present too. It's good enough to count for both."

He set out through the maze of deserted corridors. He was glad he was a little bit forward of her; it hid his unsuppressible smile from her. She'd love this, she'd go crazy over it. She'd owe him gratitude for life. It was well worth the risk of breaking northpoint drylock and trespassing in the North Reaches. "Are you brave enough to have a little adventure?" he asked.

"I don't much like the sound of that, Mart," she said. "Last time you said that was the time you found a way to bug the amity rooms. Sneaky and mean besides."

Last time hadn't made Ella like him any better. This time would do the trick. This time she'd finally realize what he thought of her. What he felt. Boy, what he felt!

He turned and gave her a thumbs-up sign, complete with cowboy grin and aw-shucks shrug. "All part of our education," he said, but worried a bit. She was clutching her elbows as if cold, and nibbling on the corner of her mouth.

But she looked wonderful as well as nervous. Waiting for the elevator, she had tucked her hands inside her sash as if into high-stitched pockets. The sash around her waist was embroidered with a copper thread that caught the light and dotted it in tiny glints around her. The seashell swung against her tunic. Then she ran her fingers through her dark curls at her temples, and whistled a tuneless hiss of worry. Her hands were restless in her anxiety, but they'd be given work to do before long, and work they'd enjoy.

The look of her filled him with courage. Initiative. A great appetite for disobedience—what the Elders called deviltry. And he was also filled with that longing: to make her like him, or to turn her liking into something a little more potent.

When the time came, he found he had no reason to worry about Ella's nerve. She joined him in the breaking of drylock without a single comment. She slipped quietly over the threshold, out of the Utility Belt and into its off-limits collar of densely packed storerooms, cells, ramps, catwalks, and tunnels, and she only made one remark: "Mart, you got guts." Suddenly he knew she was telling the truth, because his guts began to twist and ache at the compliment.

Ella *felt* like a criminal, whether Mart knew it or not. But she'd stopped being nervous. She tugged her collar up to her ears like a glamorous spy. Exciting, dangerous as it was, it was a game, too. She practiced looking slinkily out of the corners of her eyes. A dark-skinned Mata Hari. *Beauty and cunning were her weapons. No man was immune to her charms.* She began to hum a background melody: secret agent theme music.

Fifteen minutes of climbing. Then they were there, standing on a ramp in front of another cage, not un-like the dozens of cages they'd passed already, tacked into the steel fretwork of the North Reaches like cells in a beehive. But this one had a funny cloth padding inside the fencing.

Ella watched as Mart cupped his hands about the lock and put his face down close to it. "You know the Open Sesame for this place, too?" she said. Mart smiled into his hands, and the lock snapped obediently apart.

He told her to close her eyes. She did. He took her hands and moved her forward, three, four, five little steps. She could feel him almost shaking. His voice came out a little squeaky. "Now, Ella. Happy birth-day, happy C-Day, happy everything. Look."

21

She didn't even see it at first. Her eyes took time to adjust to the gloom. The bulb gave only a dingy light. But then the shape in the center of the cage suddenly became legible—a paramour, an illicit lover waiting to be touched. For the first time in her life she knew what it meant to have her heart in her throat. Her heart was almost in her blessed sinuses. Her sense of play-acting dropped away.

Mart stood in silence, and said at last, "It's a piano."

She nodded. "Saints and angels. Is it in tune?"

He shrugged.

She moved forward. It was a spinet with the full eight octaves—real ivory keys, not that plastic kind she remembered from childhood. The keys were chipped like beggars' teeth, yellowed and crazed, and as soft to touch as skin. The keyboard's protective cover had been lifted, but only recently—there wasn't any dust on the keys. She reached down and touched middle C with one hand. The other hand made an octave of F's. But she didn't press the keys.

Mart stacked a couple of cartons before the thing to serve as a piano bench. She set herself down cautiously, as if entering a boiling bath. She couldn't bring herself to look at the whole thing at once. Mart hung back for as long as possible, with his fingers working out patterns on his forearms.

"Play it," he said.

She suddenly turned and said, "Mart. What you've done!" He stood aside from her, smiling, his lip going up in the funny way that exposed a bit of gum and

22

seemed suspiciously like a sneer. But she knew he was proud: He returned her stare unflinchingly, leaning forward a bit, his blue-gray eyes eager and uncompromised. "Go on!" he said. "Let's not make this the Final Ecstasy of Ella Mencken. Try it out. Warm it up. Tickle them ivories. Give it a run for its money."

Why has he done this for me? she wondered, and said to herself: I can figure that out later. Now, face this instrument and use it.

But it'd been too long since she'd been able to sit right down and plunge into a prelude and fugue, an étude or a sonatina. She'd lost the nerve. It was too bold an action. She tried to lay both hands on the keys. The hands sank through the air as if through five inches of black water; when they had set themselves in place the blood was pounding so hard in her eyes that she could barely see.

"They'll hear it," she said in a low voice.

"Haven't you noticed my soundproofing? Stolen blankets, floor to ceiling," said Mart, and made a gesture with his hand, directing her eye around. Attached with ropes, the blankets hung several thicknesses deep on all sides. "Not a care in the world. Play as loudly as you can."

She tried to stall. "Mart, I can't tell you what this means. Ever since the music computer console burned up three years ago, I've had nothing in my head but the memories of the tapes my dad used to have, or the pieces I used to practice. I've replayed them in my mind, endlessly, with no variation. Something gets in my mind and drives me crazy, I can't get it out—like that Hornpipe from *Water Music*. There's no antidote for me. I can't sing very well, and the choir stinks, as you know—"

"Stop yapping," said Mart happily, "and start playing. I know all that stuff about you. Why do you think I brought you here?"

Finally she touched an A and released it immediately. The note rang in the muffled cage like the musical clank of a spoon falling on a metal floor. She touched the note again, and sustained it, adding a B and an E. The sound of royalty, a stamp of medieval pomp. She inverted it twice, and her left hand picked up the chord and unraveled it into a drumming triplet. She stamped and unraveled all up the keyboard and down again. The cluster of three tones was enough.

Mart asked her for a tune. She couldn't play one.

She tried to say why and failed, so played instead the same notes until finally she let her hands drop into her lap. "Mart, how'd you find this? This is like a miracle. It's as good as going home, or almost. You've given me so much."

He looked shy as he stood there trying to look at ease. A shred of dust from their northbound climb was hanging off his head like a feather. "I came out through drylock a long time ago," he said. "It's a cinch once you've figured out the equations and the schedule. I've been scouting around up here for fun—but really, finding this piano was an accident."

"And how did you learn to break the code of this cell's lock?"

24

"Once I saw the piano in there, I saw the possibilities. I had a little battery light with me, looked at the lock pretty carefully. Sneaked around in the data closet until I found the right entry."

"Just for this. You could have gotten in serious trouble."

"Tell me something I don't know. It was worth it, Ella. I had visions of climbing up here with you, and hearing you play. Sitting at your pianoside."

She felt herself stiffen a bit. She'd played nothing, and he'd kept a cautious distance. What was all this about?

"The problem is," he said, "if we don't leave soon we'll be late for school. Now that you know it's here, though, we can come back again, any time you want. Give you time to really indulge in your music."

And what would Sorb think if he found out that she and Mart were having such an adventure without him? Though Mart in his blondness shone like a jet of gas in the shadows, it was an imprint of Sorb in her thoughts that affected her strongly: his dark and glossy hair, and liquid brown eyes, his way of moving gently, as if being blown by a wind. A boy like a sail, every zephyr that meant anything to him apparent on his face.

"What's the matter?" said Mart.

"I'm just so grateful," she said smoothly.

Then she stood and pushed herself away from the piano, and that movement became a pushing toward Mart. They didn't know who reached out first, but they were quickly, anxiously kissing each other, glad and greedy and generous all together. For once, Ella's internal orchestra lost track of its current fixation, the Hornpipe in F, which lapsed into a foggy and blissful silence.

5/ Episode

Was it a plague, was it a gift? The night had been more exhausting than the day. Again and again Sorb started with the unsettling knowledge that an angel was visiting him. Giving him memories he shouldn't possess. Giving him ideas too large to carry out. Or were they?

As he spent the day thinking about what to do for Episode—it was his turn—thoughts of another recent dream kept coming back to him. He was leaving Manila, he was flying on a commercial jet. He was lifting off an island complicated with a maze of overbuilt streets and alleys, a labyrinth of confusion. He was in the air over the sea, and the sun was on his wings.

But this wasn't his memory; he'd never been to Manila. His mother had, many times; she was born there. How could a memory of hers come springing into his mind?

Springing up into the air. Sun on wings. Light on

wings. Air on wings. Angels in the air. Oh, what a tangle of desires and fears, all pressing urgently on him from the inside: to *do* something. Not just wait. Not just listen and watch. Get something *going.*

After supper, the adults were cooing over their cups of tea and larmer, dragging chairs noisily across the steel-plated floor to form a circle. Sorb watched them, to avoid thinking about Ella.

The room was so drab: slightly corroded creamy-gray plastic walls, mottled with a rash that made them look as if they'd contracted measles. A dozen identical chairs. The unalterable views set in the windowpanes—a Rocky Mountain spectacular, a Cape Cod dawn, earthrise over the moon settlement—had all faded in the monochromatic hazes of sugary blue. But the common area was a good place to watch people, at least. Even after all this time, the eleven people with whom Sorb lived on a regular basis were like exotic beasts to him . . . especially when he didn't want to think about anything else.

About Ella.

And after he had given her his seashell, too. Treasure of treasures! His mother had brought that home from a business trip, made a big deal of it.

Just abandon it. Let it go, let it slide away.

He would watch plump Mem Lotus. There she was, in her frivolous bangles, arguing with little Margaret Prite. Margaret was six. She'd squirreled her way into Mem Lotus's favorite chair and wouldn't budge. Margaret turned her dumpling cheeks up to Mem Lotus, puffed them up with air, and made a farting noise through her lips. Mem Lotus shook her bangles at Margaret in fake fury and took a chair across the way.

Or he would watch Mem Dora, Margaret's mother. She was the only citizen of the Colony who had arrived with an international reputation. She sat deep inside it, like a wealthy woman in her furs, pretending that there was nothing unusual about her. She'd been a singer once, they said, a jazz great. She never so much as chirped a note now, but the haughty look on her face would give her away in a crowd.

Or he'd watch simple Mem Troy. She was trotting out her afghan and unraveling it. Equipped for who knows how many years with only six skeins of yarn (three each of black and blue), she crocheted for hours on end, pulled it out, and began again. She looked as if she were settling comfortably under a soft puffy bruise, which she picked at with grisly interest.

They were almost convened. Jefferson Compound housed eight adults, two teenagers—himself and Ella—and two children. Everyone was there except Ella. Margaret was arranged happily in her chair, kicking at it with nervous energy, and the baby, Andrew, was already rocked to sleep and laid in his portable cradle on the table.

"Come on, Sorb, stop dawdling, curfew'll be here before we start!" said Mon Gorky. "Get yourself some tea and larmer and get over here. Ella, look sharp now! We're waiting."

Ella came from her cubicle, eyes down, seashell flagrantly displayed on her worn flannel nightshirt.

Sorb had a sense that her eyes must be heavy as lead, pitched carefully away to avoid human contact. She had avoided him since this morning. But why?

He went to the sideboard and took up a cup. Against common sense, he was cutting out larmer for a while. So what if it guarded against infection, so what if it was a daily staple—it had been giving him headaches, he was sure of it. So he made a pretense of adding it and then moved back to the circle, taking the only available seat. Next to Ella, whose hands ringed her own cup rigidly.

Under the buzz of the others' conversations he whispered, "What's the matter? You got the birthday blues? You were awfully quiet in class today. Did you go to the infirmary this morning? You sick?"

"Nah," she said, not looking over, "just thinking. That's all."

Thinking, especially on a birthday, might mean the Dead. Despite the situation his hand reached out and linked with hers, whether she wanted it or not. With soft pressure he willed himself to draw in any stink or sting of time gone by. Could spirit pass between clean dry skins, or did there always need to be a mingling of fluids? He was getting giddy with the dry heat of her fingers in his palm—or with the spirits he'd welcomed in from her. He told himself to sit and listen and keep his mind from spinning out these gusty visions. And then she gently pulled her hand away.

"Well, Sorb?" said Elder Saint Gabriel, bossy as usual.

Sorb rolled his shoulders up once or twice, imagining the weight of wings on his back, and launched himself into an experiment.

"I'm going to tell a story I read in the public access terminal," he said. "It's sort of old-fashioned so I don't know if Margaret will understand it."

"I will," promised Margaret.

"It's called 'The Lottery.'" Sorb leaned forward, capping his knees with his hands, using his eyes to stitch the group together into a single circle. He was good at it, he knew that; he enjoyed it. Even Mem Dora, who kept herself so aloof, allowed her eyes to meet his and her expression to reveal interest.

He spun out the story of the rural village gathering for a day's ritual festivities. Here and there he substituted names of folks from the neighboring compounds, just to keep Margaret involved. The villagers gathered to select stones from a box in a private ceremony, and when it was finally revealed who had ended up with the solitary black stone, the other villagers turned on her and began to throw rocks at her. To kill her.

"Yuck, an awful story!" complained Mem Waterhouse. "That's not the end, is it?"

"That's the end of *that* story," said Sorb neatly. "You can fill in for yourself whether she escaped the attack by her neighbors or not."

"Of course she did!" cried Margaret.

"Hardly suitable for children, Sorb," murmured Elder Saint Gabriel.

"I'll decide that," said Margaret's mother, Mem Dora, with a characteristic sharpness of tone.

"It is a terrible story," Sorb agreed, "but a good

31

one at the same time, don't you think? You keep thinking this poor woman is going to get something good, and then you're surprised by what really happens to her. But really, what I'm more interested in is the idea of the lottery. We could have a lottery here."

"To win what?" said Mem Lotus. "Death?"

The others began to protest. Sorb noticed Ella leaning forward, and her quiet remark, "Hear him out, it's his turn at Episode, after all," had its little effect. He continued, grateful for her attention on him.

"The thing is," he said, "that that woman didn't think the whole idea of the lottery was very good, but she didn't question it in time. She was going to be killed because she didn't open up her mouth until it was too late."

"So?" said Mem Waterhouse.

"I just keep thinking about why the Council of Elders doesn't let us out of here," said Sorb. "I was thinking we could have a lottery. Not for death, for life. Right here, right now. We could elect someone to go to them and get some answers about it."

"I can answer any questions you have, Sorb," said Elder Saint Gabriel with a huff. "I am as valid a member of the Council as any other, you know."

"I mean answer questions *publicly*," said Sorb, "you know, so they can be published in the news sheets and people can read about them. Think about the answers."

"This is getting a bit far afield from Episode, I think," said Elder Saint Gabriel with a bullying harumph. Sorb slid smoothly by as if he didn't notice.

"Not really. It's all based on the story. We're just acting out the story, that's all. We all know that nobody wants to go on the record as being too nosy."

"You're being simplistic, Sorb. You're too bright for that."

"No, really. Think of Garner Jones."

Garner Jones: dead and in the chiller these past two years. He'd been only a year or so older than Sorb and Ella when he went crazy—or so they called it. Yelling and screaming one night in the gallery, breaking curfew. Calling for *answers*, calling for *reasons*, calling for *accountability*. The j-guards had bundled him off for a lisopress treatment, an electrical-chemical therapy designed to neutralize antisocial behavior. Garner Jones had lived for a couple of months, a useless, brainless hulk, and then died of the lisopress—first fatality ever.

Not long after that, the Elders had voted in the mandatory dosage of larmer, which had medicinal qualities and reduced anxiety. True, it tasted like slightly off chicken stock dissolved in water, but there had been no threat to the social fabric since the untimely death of Garner Jones.

Who must be living still in the memories of those sitting around the common area, if their expressions were any proof. Sorb waited for a minute, for the idea to take hold, and then said softly, "We're all a little afraid of being blamed for asking too many questions—like Garner Jones. But we could pool our questions, and invent a lottery to choose someone to ask them. Then no single one of us will have to bear the brunt of being thought too inquisitive. Doesn't that make sense?"

"Garner Jones was an extreme case," said Elder Saint Gabriel.

"But he's been the *only* case in a long time," said Ella, catching on to Sorb's idea. "I think it's a great notion. I'll contribute a question: Why do we have to have j-guards when there isn't any likelihood of our being invaded?"

She turned to Mem Troy on her right. "Your turn."

Never the picture of raging curiosity, Mem Troy said, "I don't have any questions."

"Nor I," said her husband quickly.

One by one the adults declined to join in. Mem Dora didn't bother to say anything at all. Margaret alone added to the pool of inquiries; she said, "How many days till C-Day? And how will Santa Claus find us? That's my question." And when the circle had come back round to Sorb, he simply shrugged.

"So you all want to play by the regular rules," he said.

"They work," said Elder Saint Gabriel gently. "They keep the peace. No one's jumpy with extravagant hopes. You've got good ideas, Sorb, but they're somewhat misguided."

"Well, that's all the ideas I have tonight," he said abruptly, and got up and left the room. He sat on his cot and backed himself up against the wall, so hard that he almost hurt himself. There were no wings on his back, and his ideas, apparently, couldn't fly either. At least not yet.

6/ Apology

Ella stirred, scratched her elbow, and gave up on counting sheep.

Sitting up in the savage dark, she felt an unaccountable wave of—something—flicker through her poisonously. Remorse, fear, some nameless chill.

It was the not being sure that was getting to her. Pleasure, or poison? Was she gasping in memory of the impossible tenderness of mouth on mouth? Or Mart's sudden turning into Mister Romance? Did she like it, did she hate it? Or was she gasping at the shocking loss of Mart as simple Cowboy Kid, friend and ally, lab partner and innocent prankster?

His hands had been frightened, clamped on her shoulders as if he'd needed support, but his lips had emptied secrets into her mouth.

She found herself putting her feet to the steel floor, and saying to herself, *So what, so what,* to the irritating buzz of realization that it was against law and custom for residents to visit each other's cubicles during curfew. *So what, so what.*

At the door of Sorb's cubicle she paused briefly and thought—I already broke the law twice today anyway. Breaking curfew this morning, breaking drylock with Mart and going to the North Reaches. This is more of the same.

She softly tugged the door open. Sorb's breathing was gentle, like the dropping of sand onto sand by the wind at the seashore. She hated to disturb that small breeze of breath. "Sorb," she said in a whisper. "Sorb. It's Ella."

He didn't wake up.

To speak louder would be to risk waking the others.

She sat on the cold floor of his cubicle and leaned against the metal bedstead. The red curfew light from the common area came in from behind her, lit the soft skin drawn over his eyes, picked out the hair of his eyebrows. Even in sleep his dark shiny hair looked perfectly combed, straight, polite. "Sorb," she said again, touching his back-flung hand.

"Mmmm," he said. He rolled over and muttered, "Finish the ladder," and then opened his eyes.

"It's Ella."

"What's the matter?"

"Shh. I just came to say—" She should have thought out what she was going to say. She couldn't tell him about Mart *or* the piano. "I'm sorry for being so aloof today. I didn't mean to. I was just in a funny frame of mind."

"Where'd you go this morning?"

36

"Just—to be away for a little while. You know how it is."

He touched her hand. He spoke slowly, with long pauses, as if words were coming to him with difficulty. "You'll get in trouble here."

"I'm not staying."

"How's your—frame of mind—now?"

She smiled, although with the light coming from behind her Sorb probably couldn't see. "It hurts," she said. "It's okay, though."

"You can always tell me."

"I know." She believed him, too. But she didn't know how, this time. He'd be so hurt. "You're my friend, Sorb. Don't mind me when I'm moody. Just blame me out loud and I'll snap out of it."

"What's moody?" he said. "Come on, come closer."

"No. I'm going back."

He smiled, but at the odd angle of his head the smile looked more like a wince. "Sorb," she said, "that's the most interesting Episode we've had in months. So what if they wouldn't bite. Don't let it get you down."

"I *am* down, I *live* down," he said. "How much farther *down* can you be than where we are?"

"I don't know," said Ella. "What did you say about a ladder?"

"A ladder?"

"You said, 'Finish the ladder' or something when I came in."

"Oh." He closed his eyes and opened them again. "I was dreaming."

She raised her eyebrows.

He nodded. "Yeah. Strange, isn't it? I haven't dreamed in years. Till lately."

"Well, I won't tell anyone." She leaned forward suddenly and touched her lips to his forehead, and pulled away. "There. Go back to your dreams. I'm going to sleep. All's well, right?"

Sorb smiled, puckered his lips and kissed the air at her, and closed his eyes.

He seemed to drift off into sleep almost immediately. She stood and watched with a possessive, almost clinical attention. Would he start to talk in his sleep again? And how could he be dreaming?

The moisture on his lips was exaggerated by the glow of red light. His lips seemed frighteningly magical, part animal and part blossom. She had an urge to go forward and touch his lips with her finger, or to see if his smooth sallow skin was as soft as it looked. She almost did it. But she was caught still in amazement at her own daring, and then the time for it had passed, so she slipped away.

7/ C-Day

Ella had been ignoring him, no question.

It only bothered Mart a little, so far. He was as amazed as blazes himself at what had happened in the Reaches. He'd pictured things right up to the keyboard, but beyond that there'd been only a salty blankness in his imagination.

Which was now filled with a repertoire of sighs and tossings of the head. Filigreeings together of curly loops of dark hair and arching spikes of blond. Juice of two mouths. The elements of that memory had gotten all disturbed with each other and the time sequence of sensations was completely out of whack.

He'd tried once, and only to himself, to make a joke out of it. Picturing Ella at the piano, he said, "We made beautiful music together." But that joke was an insult somehow, as much to him as to her, and he scratched it out of his brain, and waited for her to show she was ready to talk to him again, to keep going.

And then, without much hoopla, came C-Day. So Mart wasn't surprised to see Ella at his compound. She looked like a holiday candle herself, dressed in red, a plaid ribbon in her curls. She had a little present of her own making—a hand-stitched pouch for him to carry computer access keys in. "Since you seem to be the world authority on it," she said. "Just promise me you won't get yourself in trouble digging in confidential files. I'd hate to think I was encouraging bad behavior."

Mart said, "I'm not out to steal any secrets. It's all a game to me, you know that." He tried to be grateful for the gift, but he really couldn't get very excited about C-Day in general. He was just glad to see *her.* "It's another example of the Great Language Lie in this place," he complained, when Ella and he went out for a walk in the Utility Belt, which was largely deserted because of the holiday. "No one can even say Christmas or Chanukah with any faith or sincerity anymore. It's just C-Day, a weak nothing of a name for a holiday. And nobody believes in it anyway."

"Sure they do," said Ella. "Mem Waterhouse ignores the secularity of the name, and decorates the door of her cubicle with cutouts from the Bible she brought in with her."

"Whippy whoopie wow," said Mart.

"Don't be nasty, it's not in the proper spirit."

"Put me in the holiday mood," he said, and draped his arms around her shoulders. "Mmmm-mm."

"Don't," she said.

"Why not, there's no one around."

She shucked his arms off, though she kept a little hold on his sleeve so as not to break away completely. "And you gave me that piano visit as a birthday–C-Day present. Guess you believed in it enough for that."

"No, I knew *you* would, that's all."

"If you're not much interested in C-Day, then I suppose I can change the subject?"

"Does it involve me and you?"

"And Sorb."

"I don't think we're ready for a threesome yet—"

"Don't be so lewd, Mart, it's C-Day. And this is serious."

"Okay," he said, wanting to humor her. Wanting to get his arms back around her. Let her get the gossip about Sorb off her mind and then he'd wheel things back to where he wanted them.

Ella sighed and said, "You know, Sorb had a great idea the other night during Episode." She described the story of the lottery and how Sorb thought it could work for them. Mart only half heard her remarks; his ears were filling up at the same time with the sound of her high regard for Sorb. She carried him around with her, set him there between them even when they were out for a romantic stroll. It made him grit his teeth and chew on the inside of his lips, but for the sake of C-Day he decided to try to squelch his annoyance.

"Sorb's always been full of big ideas," he said, aiming at a noncommittal tone. "Remember the time he put on that play about Garner Jones during the Day

Six assembly? He'd signed up to do a report on the life cycle of the acemyte plant, and he stood there with a head of acemyte and said, 'This is a vegetable known as Garner Jones.' People didn't know whether to laugh or scream."

"You're not listening. What do you think of his idea?"

"Oh, Ella, it's just Sorb soaring off again. What's wrong with how the Council of Elders works? So they're a little bossy, so what? You notice anyone complaining?"

"Well, I notice Sorb complaining," said Ella, in a voice which meant she noticed Mart *not* complaining.

"You want me to be huffy and puffy and offended by everything?" he said. "I'm just not, is all. They don't bother me, I don't bother them. What's wrong with that?"

"What's wrong with that," said Ella, "is the vegetable known as Garner Jones. What happens if there is a vegetable known as Mart Rengage? How do you feel about it then?"

"Then I *don't* feel about it," he said simply, admiring his own cleverness. "Now what I feel about you is a different story." And out went his arm again, a loop around her shoulders.

But she didn't warm up to him, holiday spirit or no, and when he said good-bye to her later on he was in a foul mood at Sorb, and at her, and everyone else who came into his mind.

Walking back to Jefferson, Ella was relieved to be apart from both Mart and Sorb for a while. She stopped in the lavatory and washed her hands, simply to prolong the pleasure of being alone. She looked at herself in the mirror and thought: Ella Mencken, how can you find out how you really feel about them? The Ella Mencken looking back at her, self-conscious and proud, familiar for a while and then shockingly strange to her, had no answers.

Mart's big present to her—the secret of the piano—had thrown her situation into high contrast. She knew Mart was fond of her, maybe even loved her, and that his gift to her was a genuine gift. Given out of love and friendship.

True, she thought music was a private thing, at least here in the Colony. There was so little that *was* private; if music couldn't be your own language, from and to yourself, then what could? But it also seemed to her that Mart's generous and courageous gift was a kind of bribe, and now she felt pressured to respond to him. To love him merely in gratitude for returning music to her life.

Maybe it *was* love, this resistance to Mart, this attraction to him. There was a tantalizing aspect of giving in—and then resisting temptation. Was it love? If so, was this all it was: a light roasting of the skin of her heart? But the deep inside core of her remained unstamped by these games, and took nothing from him, really. Well, she didn't mind the delirium of kisses and caresses. But wasn't love supposed to be more than that, wasn't it the thing that touched you at your most central stem?

She turned off the water. She was being wasteful. In the mirror, Ella Mencken folded her arms determinedly and said, "You've got to find out. That's your job."

And finding out meant what she felt about Sorb, too. Sorb, who could turn a boring Episode into a racing exercise in democracy. Sorb, who could grin like a practical joker and then twist your heart by a question no one could answer. Was it love, or merely respect? Was she simply jealous of his being able to dream?

Heading back to the compound, she began to imagine asking people: How do you know if you're in love? She chuckled at the thought. The older men in the Pioneer Colony seemed to feel nothing, dense and dull as concrete pillars. And so many of the women like that, too. And then some of the women who would drag her down into gossip and nonsense. Like dear Mem Lotus, who would flutter around and drag out every cliché in the book, romanticizing beyond belief.

There was only Mem Dora Prite, silent, severe, proud. She had had that famous love affair and marriage with Senator John Prite. She lived behind a scowl, and never spoke of him, or of her old life. Never opened her mouth to sing. She just took care of little Margaret, who danced about in her red corduroy overalls, apparently unaware that her mother was lacking in human warmth.

One day, maybe, she'd ask Mem Dora. If she ever got up the nerve.

Just before Episode, Mem Lotus announced a surprise. First she swore everyone to secrecy, and she

44

said to Elder Saint Gabriel that if he let any of this slip to the Council she'd make life so miserable for him he'd wish he were dead. They watched Elder Saint Gabriel hem and stall, unwilling to sanction illegal behavior, till Mem Lotus said he could damn well go out to the gallery if he didn't want to take part. So he relented. Then Mem Lotus went into the food station and pulled a box from one of the top shelves.

"I got up one night last week, at two in the A.M., and I made these, even though those stupid night-lamps cast so little light that I could hardly read the markings on the measuring cups. I used up two weeks of sugar rations, I'll announce it right now, and I'll suffer for it myself. I don't care. Eat up and have a good time."

They were Christmas cookies. Overweight angels, lopsided bells, six-pointed stars. ("For you, Mon Gorky," said Mem Lotus largely.) They were coated with a sugar dusting, four dozen cookies in the box. Very beautiful, very illegal. Mem Lotus could be marched before the Council of Elders for misappropriation of sugar.

But nobody raised an eyebrow. Elder Saint Gabriel took a bell and pretended to ring it; he was so seldom playful that it was almost unbearably funny. Mem Lotus told the whole elaborate story of how, lacking cookie cutters, she'd used a knife to carve the shapes out of the dough. Margaret, who had never had a cookie before, wanted to save hers.

Then Ella said, "Now, Mem Dora, since it's C-Day, will you sing us a carol?"

45

"No, I don't think so, Ella," said Mem Dora. "You sing one for us."

"For goodness' sake, don't be a spoilsport on C-Day too!" said Mem Lotus, carried away with the success of her cookies. "We all know perfectly well you have convictions. But this is C-Day. Who knows how many more we'll have together?"

Ella watched her. Mem Dora broke the points off a cookie star and said haughtily, "You know how I feel about it. It doesn't do any good to ask me." How could such a beautiful woman look so high and mighty and mean? There she stood, smaller than Ella, small as an old woman although she couldn't be more than forty. Her hair, boisterous marine-black loops, was bound by a ribbon running from the nape of her neck around her forehead and down the other side, tied at the back. Her skin, the creamiest brown, glistened with a sudden sweat.

"Oh, come on." That was Sorb. "It'd be such a treat. Just this once."

"Paul and Silas sang in prison," observed Mem Waterhouse helpfully. "And their chains were snapped in two. Acts 16:25–26, if I remember—"

"I won't sing," said Mem Dora again, and her voice shook. "Just leave me alone. Please."

"All right, all right, don't make an interplanetary case out of it," snorted Mem Lotus. "Forget it, Ella, all right? Selfish is selfish to the end."

The holiday C-Day mood trailed away into regular everyday petulance. As the adults began to get their tea and larmer ready, Ella watched Mem Dora excuse herself from the group and go into her cubicle. Shut the door.

Then she turned and caught a glimpse of Sorb—Sorb noticing everything, Sorb taking it all in. Ella shrugged her shoulders and mouthed words across the space between them: "Hark the herald angels won't sing."

"Fa la la la la, la la la la," Sorb sang out loud to her.

8/ The Glass Garden

A few days later, when Ella went to the glass garden
for her Day Five assignment as nursery aide, a man
she didn't know well was waiting at the door with a
key and a note. "Mem Gesevich isn't feeling up to par
this afternoon. She says good luck and don't let a
j-guard get a foot in the door." He smiled and ambled
away.

> Dear Ella,
>   Sorry to do this to you with Glenn in sick bay,
> and the kids have been acting so wild lately. I
> hope you can hold down the fort. Keep the outer
> shades drawn and you be careful of j-guards,
> okay? Tell him it's quasiquarantine, it's naptime,
> anything, if he actually comes. Me, I'm sipping
> orange water and urinating every 7 minutes—it's
> one of these bugs that's only drowned by running
> fluids all day through the system. Good luck +
> Happy N. Year! Mem Gesevich.

Ella put the key in the door. The bolt slid with a gritty tremor, and she passed it back and forth twice more, for the fun of it. It was an antique lock—the iron bolt shuttled in and out of the jamb with such simplicity. It reminded her of everything in the past that was being forgotten, the good old *feel* of things.

But no time to stand and gape. With Mem Gesevich absent today, there was a lot of work to be done.

She moved about the glass garden, pleased to be alone for a few minutes, pleased to be responsible. Mem Gesevich was an old mother hen who treated Ella as if she were only marginally older than the toddlers. She ruled the roost, that was the saying— standing up to j-guards at every intrusion, taking no nonsense from interfering parents. Hardly ever being sick, either; today was a first.

Ella set out the chairs for the little ones, and worried about how the children would respond to Mem Gesevich's absence. There were only seven children now, since Glenn Trenton was in sick bay and Rebecca Moyer had died and been put in the chiller. The kids were excitable; Ella's usual role was as pacifier, quiet friend. She'd have to be calm and authoritative today, look capable of being in charge.

But before the kids arrived, Ella allowed herself to do something she'd always wanted: to stand on a desk and look out the glass walls, which gave the place its name, out to the larger hall used for the harvesting of acemyte. Over the opaque paneling Ella could see the harvesting crew working its way along the trays. Folks dipped their hands in the water, adjusting nutri-

49

ent pipes and torpa lights. And along came Mem Nazira Afshar with the first arrival.

Baby Andrew in his portable crib. Then Mon Ackerholm with his identical twin toddlers, Glenda and Belinda. Mon X'an with beautiful silent Tachi. In his old-fashioned wheelchair, Charles Trualt, propelling himself. He saw that Mem Gesevich was missing, and spoke like a civic official—"We are truly sorry for this turn of events"—and then he burst into tears. Finally, Mem Mbulu with her own child, Sam, and Sam's cousin, Abraham.

It would be important to keep the regular routine. The kids could be wild and alarmed by small changes. Ella saw to it that they set out their small lunch tubs around the table, returned to find their photomatrices in the pile and stick them up on the felt board, and then take their places again. She moved quickly through the identification bit—pointing to each photomatrix and asking them who was missing. They all looked around soberly—before lunch they were never very quick or sociable—and Ella had to prod them. "It's Glenn. Remember, Glenn is in sick bay. He'll be back in a couple of days, if he's feeling better."

Abe and Sam consulted each other and Abe said, "And there's Rebecca gone, too. 'Member?"

A couple of others echoed Rebecca's name but hollowly: It had a nice sound, it meant something but they couldn't remember what. Ella acknowledged Rebecca's continued absence, and reminded them that Mem Gesevich was gone, too, and then she led them in the lunch song.

50

"Here we are together, together, together.
Here we are together in the afternoon class."

Then Ella sat down at the small table and opened
her tub, and the kids wrestled with theirs. Ella could
barely eat for telling them to stay seated, all except
Charles, of course, who still wept for Mem Gesevich and wouldn't touch his carrot cubes or nutro-
brittle.

As the kids ate, they became more chatty—letting
off volleys of nonsense syllables which were taken up
in chorus, automatically, by the others—coming out
then with little bursts of information about their various compounds—and, finally, beginning real conversation with each other. It was as if they had to learn
anew every day who they were and how to be together, Ella reckoned. It was a hard thing for them
to learn, apparently.

Belinda was the first to whoop away from the table
and head for the puppets, and Glenda followed dis-
mally behind, squatting a few feet away from where
Belinda was making her selection. "You can have one,
too, Glenda," called Ella, but as always Glenda pre-
ferred to watch her sister. The puppets were a sorry
lot, nothing like the bristled, padded, eyelashed crea-
tures Ella could remember from her childhood in Boston urb. These were old threadbare socks, tediously
alike, with red flannel tongues and scrap-material
eyes, prepared with careful stitches by old women in
the compounds.

"This be Witch Woman," announced Belinda, transforming a sock into an arch-necked creature. "Witch

51

Woman to the rescue. Whee!" Witch Woman plunged at Glenda and hit her on the forehead.

Ella stopped that, cleared up the tubs, except for those of Charles and Tachi, who hadn't eaten enough yet, and she set the others to a fast-paced march around the glass garden. Two by two: Belinda and Abe, Glenda and teetering Sam. Witch Woman led the way like a figurehead. Abe, Glenda, and Belinda chanted a nursery rhyme.

"Here we go 'round the mulberry bush,
The mulberry bush, the mulberry bush.
Here we go 'round the mulberry bush
So early in the morning."

When it came near to naptime, she gathered the kids around the story corner and told them a story, and was glad to be free of the studying gaze of Mem Gesevich, for once.

"Once upon a time, in a colony far away, there lived a king and a queen, who gave birth to a lovely baby girl, named Sleeping Beauty. The king and queen invited all their friends to the compound for a birthday party, but one wicked old woman they forgot to invite."

"Witch Woman," said Belinda.

"Yes indeed," said Ella, feeling Glenda draw nearer. "It was Witch Woman. She found out about the party and she dressed all in black, and she stormed through the colony and arrived at the compound just as the presents were being given."

"What did the baby get?" asked Tachi.

"Toys," said Belinda.

"Germs," said Abe. "Babies always get germs. That's what Mem Mbulu say. Sam gots germs."

"She got socks," said Charles. "Boring socks."

"She got pills," said Glenda. "Right?"

"Right," said Ella. "The baby was given a pill to be healthy, and a pill to be pretty, and a pill to be smart, and a pill to be strong. One by one she swallowed those pills, easy as pie."

"What's *pie*?" said Abe, as if it were objectionable even without a definition. He liked the way he said it and said it again. "What's *pie*?"

"Easy as water," said Ella. "But then Witch Woman arrived and—do you know what happened then?"

"She huffed and she puffed and she blowed the place in!" screamed Belinda. They all huffed and puffed for a while. Ella let them go on, and when they had quieted, said, "No. She gave the baby a pill to make her fall asleep. And when Sleeping Beauty fell asleep, so did the queen and so did the king. And old Witch Woman raced as fast as she could go down the hall, out of that place, because one by one all the friends were falling asleep. Everybody in the whole compound fell asleep. And they never woke up."

She sat there, not moving a muscle. The kids sat still and stared at her. Charles drummed his fingers on the tray of his wheelchair, and Abe grinned and put his forefinger to his lips. They were all as still as night.

Belinda gave in first. "No!" she shouted, full of high spirits. "No! No! No!"

"No!" yelled Abe. Charles hit his tray, hard. "No,

no!" Sam threw his arms around Tachi's neck and they both sang out, "No, no, no!" Andrew stirred in Ella's arms but didn't waken. And Glenda was silent, squeezing Ella's knee so tightly that Ella imagined the kneecap coming loose like the lid of a jar.

"Okay, quiet down," said Ella, and they did so, beaming. "And well, after a hundred years a giant patch of acemyte had grown up in front of the door to the compound, so nobody even remembered that anyone was in there. But one day a brave boy went and pulled all the leaves of the acemyte off, and found the lost door behind it. He went down the dark corridor and into the dark compound. He saw everybody asleep, including the king and queen and all the friends and the little baby, Sleeping Beauty. And do you know what he did?"

They watched Abe get to his feet and solemnly step forward. He planted a kiss on the thin-haired head of Andrew.

"Absolutely," said Ella. "The brave boy kissed the little baby, and the baby woke up and started screaming for breakfast, and her screams woke up the king and the queen and all the friends. And everyone lived happily every after."

Belinda said, "But what about Witch Woman? Why didn't she just come and give the baby another pill?"

"She was in the chiller by then," said Ella.

"Witch Woman can come out of the chiller," said Belinda. "Witch Woman can do *anything.*"

"Naptime," said Ella. And without a single complaint the kids found their blankets, kissed Ella one by one, and lay down and closed their eyes. Ella adjusted the back of Charles's wheelchair to its reclining position. He looked up at her and said, "What would we do if the j-guard came?"

"You leave that to me. You love to worry," said Ella fondly. "Sleep now."

He followed her advice. Before long, Ella was able to move softly around the glass garden, arranging materials for the lessons she would attempt to hold later. The children slept as softly as sponges drifting in their cleaning fluid, intake, outgo, breath like the soft hush of a candle flame. Staunch Belinda in her sleep had moved up next to Glenda, as she always did, and slept with an arm cast over her quiet sister's shoulder. Ella felt tall as a tree, and the children were like ripe fruits, windfallen and sweetly scented, small and round on the ground below her.

When a light but insistent knock sounded at the door, Ella's thought was to collect her fruits and run. But of course that was just a dream thought: there was no place to run to. And a j-guard was just a nuisance, not a terrorist. She needn't fear Witch Woman in any guise. Still, she caught herself looking over to see if Charles had been awakened by the knock. He hadn't.

She went up close to the translucent door, unable to tell by the shape which j-guard it was. With the thought of powerful Mem Gesevich in mind, a talisman, she was ready to be horrendous. "Who's there?" she said firmly.

"Open up, Ella, quickly. It's me. Mart."

9/ New Year's Eve

He kissed her. She flinched.

"You don't be so bold," she said. "There's kids here. You want them to get the wrong idea?"

"It's the right idea," he whispered. He was looking his best, bright as blazes, as Mem Lotus was fond of saying. Ella was wary of his good looks, all blond and apparent, while she was just her quiet self. She didn't feel gorgeous enough to be with him; she might just be mean instead.

"What're you doing off your post?" she said.

"I found out the j-guard schedule, Ella. We can get out again and go north to the pie-ano. Have more time than we did last time. Can you get away later?"

She shrugged.

He said, "Come on, stop putting it off. I go through all this trouble to dig up a piano for you and you keep saying *Nah, nah.* We'll go out, have our own New Year's Eve party, why not? Won't be till midnight, of course, we'd never get through drylock after curfew—that's when they put on the heavy stuff. Now when can you get free, and don't say *No.* "

"Stop being so sexy," she said. "Don't tell me what to say. I'll say what I want."

"Well?"

"No."

IIe reached out and started fiddling with her sash, and he pouted when she pulled it away. Then his face suddenly went flat and pale, all but the gray fire eyes, and it took Ella a minute to realize why. There'd been another knock at the door.

She grabbed his hand and said, "Oh, you moron, now look! Now it's the j-guard! How'll we explain this?"

"Careful, careful," and he danced away from her on jittery feet, "just don't let him in, you didn't see me here anyway—" Underneath the glass panels by the drawing boards was a long low storage closet with a sliding door. Mart flipped the door back and scattered some balls and blocks out of the closet, and slipped himself inside. Ella just saw the door closed safely, and then she turned and went to answer the knock of the j-guard.

"Check and survey," said the vague shape outside the glass door.

"Check and survey forbidden. As usual. Orders of—"

"Come on, we've got it that Mem Gesevich isn't there. You can't stand behind her orders, toots. Open up."

57

"Orders of Mencken," said Ella. "I don't need any others."

She didn't know which j-guard it was, Mon Conway or Mon Micklersohn. Mon Conway was only a few years older than Ella; they'd been in class together a couple of years ago, after all. Mon Micklersohn was a regular troublemaker. "The kids are asleep," she said carefully, "and I'm not letting you rouse them for your lousy check and survey. We have trouble here, we'll get you on the diatone first thing. Till then, so long."

"Let me in, Ella Mencken."

She was at a loss. She'd witnessed Mem Gesevich's turning away the j-guard every day until it'd become a joke, but she couldn't recall the techniques used. If she stalled much longer, he might really search the place once he came in, and he might find Mart, here, off his post. She opened the door, saying, "Well, against my principles, Mon—"

It was Mon Conway, grinning ear to ear. She felt furious for not having stood up against him. Only three years older than she, barely a mon. She didn't feel respectful at all.

"Look, and leave," she snapped. "No waking them. Have your day in the j-guard locker room, get a big slap on the behind because you finally got into the glass garden. Go on, it's my present to you, Mon Conway. All's calm here. You see it, now get out."

He was walking about between the small tables, tramping his big ugly boots on the storytelling rug, looking at the drawings on the wall, of stick people and large acemyte clumps, lined up in a ritualistic frieze. "Guess they wouldn't be drawing trees and freehouses and the sun like we used to, would they?" he said.

Charles stirred in his wheelchair, but he hadn't the strength to raise his head by himself. "This is a day for visitors, eh?" he said.

"Charles, shush, you'll wake the others," said Ella. He must have seen Mart come in. He must know Mart was in the closet. "No talking during naptime. Do you hear me?"

"Loud and clear," he said.

Mon Conway said, "Now it's time for a report, Ella. You'll allow me that? It's on my assignment list—"

"Show-off, braggart, pighead mule," said Ella, and, maybe because Charles was listening, made it into a rhyme. "Big man enters nursery school."

The communication fork came out of the sling around Mon Conway's waist, and he adjusted some knobs and spoke into it. "Mon Conway calling, 3-X check-in. Quadrant 7, Utility Belt, the glass garden."

"Oooh la la," came the voice crackling back. "A moment in history."

"Present: Ella Mencken and seven children," said Mon Conway. "Mem Gesevich is in sick bay."

"Taking mestrol checks, Mon Conway?"

Mon Conway smiled at Ella and spoke into the fork. "The kids are sleeping. Naptime in Babyland. Ella Mencken talked me out of it."

"It's advised" came back the voice of Mon Conway's superior.

Ella put on her most stubborn expression. Mestrol checks helped to chart the progression of viruses throughout the Colony. They required a syringe to be plunged, quickly and painfully, into the armpit. While the Council of Elders had authorized the j-guards to carry out random checks at will, common practice by most of the colonists protected small children from being so violated. And on this point Ella—like Mem Gesevich, her boss—was willing to be extremely troublesome.

Mon Conway must have seen it in her face. "Advice acknowledged," he reported. "I'll check back in at 4-X."

Just before he left, he turned and said, "Well, don't take it too seriously, Ella. I didn't do the mestrol checks, after all. Don't harbor a grudge. I don't get to see kids all together like this, you know. No babes in my compound at all. I didn't hurt them."

"You win," said Ella, pretending subservience just to hurry him out of there. "Don't expect it to happen again, though."

When he'd gone, Mart crawled out of his slot and Charles said, "I knew you were there all the time. Mem Gesevich should come back, I think."

"Yeah, well, you're a good kid," said Mart. "Keep it under your hat."

"I don't have a *hat*."

"I'd better go," said Mart. "Later, Ella, come on. It's New Year's Eve, for God's sake."

"All *right*," she said, "just shut up about it, will you?" All that anger was flooding out of her now, toward Mart instead of toward Mon Conway, and then away from him because it wasn't fair, and in the wake of that confusion she'd said yes. Against her will. Now she had to go through with it because she believed in keeping her word. "Don't hammer me to death. Just go and let me get back to work."

"You are adorable," said Mart. She almost picked him up and threw him out the door.

By the time she was to meet him, she was exhausted, and her feelings less clear than ever. Resisting him was such hard work, and she didn't really want to, or not entirely. He was her friend, he was doing her a favor, he was giving her a present unparalleled in the history of the Pioneer Colony. How could she be so selfish? So cold? She was worse than Mem Dora.

Trying to be nice, she broke the ice with Mart as soon as they'd successfully crossed out of drylock and were heading north. She told him about the same old conflict happening again last night, just before Episode. Mem Lotus had gotten it into her head that Mem Dora should sing for New Year's. "She wheedled unmercifully," said Ella. "She said, 'It's the beginning of a new year, Mem Dora, day after tomorrow. Come on, don't be bashful. Sing "The Mountains of Mourne." Sing "Going Home to Crystal Earth," or "When I Get to Heaven Send Me Postcards of the Ocean," or "Auld Lang Syne" even. Don't be so greedy.' But she just wouldn't, same as always. Refused."

"Oh, you taking lessons?" said Mart, and Ella didn't get it at first. Then she said, "At being stubborn? No, I know how to do that all by myself."

She was quiet the rest of the way to the piano, however, wondering if she and Mem Dora had anything in common besides being musicians.

When they arrived, she found herself face to face with the same dilemma: Playing music for Mart was impossible for her. The keys were as docile and pliant beneath her fingers as they could be; it was her own will which wasn't pliant.

Something to do with privacy. Something to do with an inner voice that had been so long denied that it was now almost mute. Sure, she had played in public as a younger girl, but there'd also been long hours just to fool around, with no one to amuse but herself. Here she was in a concert, and she didn't want to be. Maybe it was selfish, but it was a stronger feeling than her desire to please Mart, to thank him for trying to make this possible. She didn't want to owe Mart, she didn't want music to be currency. It had to be free of that role.

"Come on," said Mart, having regained his breath after the exertion of the climb. "Shall I lie across the top of the piano and look inspiring?"

He looked inspiring already, no shortage of *that* in him. The inspiration was to weep, however.

"Play me a lullaby," he said, not understanding her hesitancy.

"It's so hard," she said. "I feel so foolish."

"I'll sit behind the piano where you can't see me.

Just play it, and the sound will come out through the back all around me, like a spraying, good as hot water and alcohol diluent."

"Go on, sit down," she said, waving her hand. When he was out of view she pressed a chord on the piano lightly, a major seventh; its poignant expectancy trapped her in a terrible, hopeless, hollow mood. She took her hands off the piano and let the notes fade, and tried to find words for how she felt. "The kids don't even know what houses and trees look like," she finally said.

Mart was silent. She could feel him waiting there for her to play. She was going to have to disappoint him. She was going to have to get up and say that it was time to go back. He would be furious, and hurt, and she could think of nothing else to do.

She heard the root note in the major seventh chord, and she dipped down to the springboard note below, and, surprising herself, she began to sing. That song she barely remembered, that had come up during Episode last night. Despite her conviction that she couldn't sing, she let the song come out of her, in whatever weak, watery fashion it would take. It wasn't quality of pitch or tone she was after, it was the sad sad sound of the song.

"Should auld acquaintance be forgot
And never brought to mind?
Should auld acquaintance be forgot,
And days of auld lang syne?
For auld lang syne, my dear,

For auld lang syne;
We'll take a cup o' kindness yet,
For auld lang syne."

She closed her eyes. The forbidden past didn't bother her. It was the future being forbidden that bothered her.

"They don't even know what trees are," she said.

PART TWO

There was ice, and howling winds.

Snowflakes as broad as an armspan whirled out of the night sky. Icicles flew like javelins through the midnight tempest, chased by their own whistling. Warmth was an idea that had not yet dawned in history.

So maybe this was a dream, or maybe not. Sorb was wandering in an ice maze, through snowbanks piled so high he couldn't see over them. The walls were the dead white of fish, with streaks of interstellar green and Attic blue faintly patterned deep inside, like striations in marble. Though he tried to peer through, he couldn't see. He stumbled, hands aching with the cold. He was hurrying, but afraid to hurry, because there was a threat stalking him in the ice maze. The danger might as well be ahead of him as behind him.

The angel of all those earlier dreams was here,

67

too, but just out of sight. He listened for the gentle racket of its wings above the hiss of wind and blowing snow, but he could detect nothing. He imagined the naked feet settling on the wall, and firm opalescent hands reaching for him—warmth in this blizzard!—and he ran toward the possibility, not knowing where it was. He couldn't awake from the dream and he couldn't credit it with much chance for success, but he ran for the winged rescuer anyway.

A pair of snowflakes like the wheeling gears of an old machine came at him from two sides in the dark, grazing his soft, beardless face. They ripped him with a painless quickness, almost before he knew what had happened, and his face on the two sides split open into two puckers of skin. Delicate as Asian silk, those wounds, and from them fell two fruits, a golden orange on the left and a pure white apple on the right. He caught them with each hand, and held the fruits up against his rippled skin.

In his hands were male and female, one in either hand. From his face had erupted the golden female and the pale male. The fruits were the gift of his mother and his father. He sniffed them—good redolent wealth of aroma, the tropical citrus tang and the cool northern snap. The scent and the warmth of the fruits healed the slashed scars on his face.

And closer and closer, in the ice maze, drew the faceless villain and the faceless angel. Sorb was motionless with the fear that he would run smack into the monster, or inadvertently slip away from the saving presence of the angel. His heels felt frozen to the slick ice floor, and the ripe fruits withered in his hands to brown twisted lumps of rot and mold. . . .

He couldn't wait in this ice prison. He had to act. Even if it brought his own death down on top of him, he had to torch this place. Burn it down. Splash a flame at the glazed impenetrability of the walls, set on fire the torment of dead ends, frozen missteps, endless waiting. Even if it brought the faceless monster onto him. Sorb rubbed his hands back and forth, inventing fire.

If he could.

10/ The Ice Maze

Waking at last, he felt instinctively to see if his cheeks were slit, but they were soft and regular and only a bit warmer than usual. His hands were chapped, but not, he saw, charred. Apparently, he hadn't been able to bring fire forth of his own accord.

As he lay there, thoughts of the past began to collect. Dangerous thoughts. Why was he dreaming so much, and about the past? He knew perfectly well that the past was supposed to be examined only during evening Episode, and even then great pains were taken to make the past amusing and instructive, never provocatively sad. *Everyone* had lost the past; to dwell on it at length was both uncharitable and immoral. You had to learn to overlook the Dead, to keep your gaze sternly on the present. It was a given.

But his dream had nearly brought back his parents. He hadn't thought of them in months. Years.

                                    *   *   *

Later that day, Sorb sat among the blips and bleeps
of the maintenance computer lab, which chirred along
doing its work with a conscientiousness he wasn't
inclined to match. His boss, Mem Wonski, was busy
filling out reports and so didn't hover in her usual
way. Sorb sat very still in his chair, letting his computer do some routine work, hoping his mind would
stretch like elastic to admit some meaning into that
dream.

Little by little.

The forbidden memory.

Approached him.

Those terrible two days in the Boston urb, at the
very end, when an early snow fell, and warnings from
the national broadcasters and the underground press
predicted a similar doom.

Sorb and his father and mother had disobeyed the
Evacuation Plan for their lottery sector number, and
they'd bribed and cheated their way onto the interdis-
trict transit line. Sorb's father had worked for Future
Research, and he knew lots of classified information
about the Pioneer Colony. He was ready with phony
datacards when the time came to run for it.

All the last day, as the snow fell and the transport
unit crawled westward, Sorb's mother had sat and
watched the gray-brown mulch settle on roads and
freehouses and the occasional sad tree. Alone of them
all, she didn't cry for life gone or for life to come; she
merely sat and watched the world on its last day. As
if it were worthy of her interest, but only until something else came along.

And the explosions didn't occur until they were streaming on foot toward Pioneer, when panic was at its height. Sorb didn't see his father fall or his mother stay to help him. He knew that was what must have happened; his father had a carmite pin in his hip which tended to give way when he moved too quickly. The blast came, and the snow had a transparency: It showed itself more brilliantly gray than ever, as if the blast had pushed right through the screen of the snow all the darkest parts of the world, normally unseen by human eyes. It was only in picking himself up from the road that Sorb realized that his parents had fallen behind.

But the Pioneer Colony loomed in his mind with devilish singularity. No more waiting or wondering; he'd run. Run like the blazes.

He'd left them behind.

The room tilted around him as he said that inside himself. *You left them behind.* And as it righted itself, slowly, he had a sudden desperate taste for larmer, to help him forget, help him relax. Help it not matter.

But it did matter, it did. And it hadn't stopped mattering, and mattered still. In his dream, he'd fumbled around in an ice maze, failing in his tries to manufacture a spark. But he *had* to try it in real life, he had to, or he'd freeze up, and forget for good.

Breaktime came, and his colleagues stood and stretched. Mem Wonski arched an eyebrow at him from across the room and called, "You're looking foggy again, Sorb. Go out and get yourself some tea and larmer—I don't want you working through your breaktime."

He wanted to sit there and think. Plan. Act. Do.

"Get on with you," said Mem Wonski.

He dragged his feet as he left.

Resting, his colleagues were enmeshed in gossip about various romances and jealousies of significant intrigue. Endless gossip, endless repeating of the same old plots. Sorb dangled his spoon in his cup of tea, and waited for a silence, and then said, "I wonder what would happen if we called for an election."

The gossip fizzled out.

"To vote on what?"

"Well," said Sorb, "we could have a couple of questions. Like how many people would like to stop doing maintenance work and set their energies toward digging us out of here instead."

"That's for the Council of Elders to decide!" The reaction was distinctly appalled.

"Well, yeah, but the Council of Elders always makes up its own agenda," mused Sorb. "What if folks presented them with a question and demanded there be a public vote on it?"

It happened that Elder Saint Gabriel was in the room, and the disgruntled workers turned to him for rebuttal. He cleared his throat and said gently, "The Council of Elders was elected by the colonists, Sorb, when we first came down here. *That's* the appropriate body to suggest such a bold idea, and it reserves the right to do so when the time comes."

"Yeah, but," said Sorb, "didn't the Council get elected with the idea that we were going to be here for two years? And now it's been almost five?"

"The Council considers such things—"

"You know, it's like a concentration camp," said Sorb, and a dozen voices protested. "No, I mean it. So we have a certain amount of freedom, we can walk here, we can walk there. But we can't get out."

"Don't you ever make that comparison," snapped Elder Saint Gabriel. "No concentration camp prisoners were ever allowed to vote for their own system of government, to make their own rules."

"But it's effectively the same thing," said Sorb, nonplussed. "We can't get out, and the Council of Elders never even brings up the question about *trying* to get out anymore. Cripes, even I remember that at first that's all we used to talk about, until the Council recommended it was better for our mental health if we didn't obsess about it all the time."

"The Council has the mental health of the colonists at heart," said Elder Saint Gabriel.

"But it squelches questioning," said Sorb. "Maybe it doesn't mean to, but it does. It ought to be possible for us to vote on how we want to spend our time. Doing tedious maintenance work? Or maybe we'd rather throw ourselves into trying to dig out the collapsed tunnels and take our chances up there. It ought to be possible, no?"

"No," said several people. "It should be for those who know best to decide."

"I don't know *best*," said Sorb, irritated, "but I

know *something*. And I think it's strange that nobody can even raise a decent *question* around here. Nobody ever does."

"The boy is right," said an older woman in a kerchief. "Even that Mem Dora used to be a firebrand, and she's still as death."

Sorb even loved the word: *firebrand*. It seemed to warm the icy water in his veins and persuade it to flow like hot blood, the way it should. But used with Mem Dora? "What do you mean?"

"She was a top-notch dissenter," said someone. "You kids are too young to know that side of her. She sure keeps it quiet here."

"Why doesn't she try to stir things up?" said someone.

"She's a mother," said someone else.

"A bad mother," said someone else.

"Every mother is a bad mother," came from the back of the room, and a dirty giggle rippled around. Things then began to lurch along in their old usual way, this time gossip about Mem Dora. What a singer she'd been, a powerhouse plus—had anyone ever heard her sing? Sorb was heartsick with the change of focus, and darting an angry glance at Elder Saint Gabriel, he got up and noisily clattered out of the room.

Back at his terminal a few minutes before break was over, he sat down and began to make a few notes.

Daddy was full of pride in his ancestry. He used to say that the Greek Jews in World War II, put into

concentration camps by the Nazis, maintained a sense of themselves through dancing. They wouldn't release their grip on life an instant before it was stolen from them. The firebrands sing, and dance, and proclaim life even in the face of death. They turn to the frozen walls and burn them down with their vitality. No matter who has died before, the firebrands jealously guard their lives, in memory, in appreciation.

Mommy, Daddy, I burn in this maze of ice. For you.

There was a sound at the door. Mem Wonski came in, followed by a couple of j-guards. "Look, your job is easy," she said to them, pointing a finger across the room at Sorb. "There he is. Go ahead."

11/ The Lisopress

Showing up at dinnertime, Mart knew, would cause fuss and flurry. Arched eyebrows and catty remarks. Each compound had only so much food allotted per meal that sharing with a visitor at mealtime was hard to bring off with any grace. But he had Ella in his taste buds, a kind of appetite and a kind of addiction, and he didn't care how her compound-mates groused.

Which they did, but Ella said Mart could eat from her dish. And Mem Lotus, in her helpful way, observed that Sorb wasn't around anyway and his portion was losing nutrition by the minute. Mart might as well eat that.

"Whose turn for Episode tonight?" asked Mon Troy, and Mem Nazira said, "It must be Ella's, that's why loverboy's here."

Mart had a spoonful of Slavic Slosh at his lips, and he took it in with a little inward whistle. He mulled over his catalog of barbed statements, but left each one unspoken, surprising himself. He didn't mind that jab from Mem Nazira. In fact, he liked it. He glanced at Ella. No telling what she thought; she was silent and her eyes downcast.

Anything to tie him to her, anything to stand as public awareness of their—their—whatever it was. Friendship? Affair? Romance? He didn't know what to call the force percolating inside him—sometimes it was just plain old lust, sometimes more, sometimes other—but even Mart, who laughed at the churchi-ness of Mem Waterhouse and the preachiness of grown-ups in general, felt a need for some official stamp of approval, or recognition, that something was going *on* between him and Ella, something was *brewing.*

Not that he wanted to get married—toads and vi-pers! Besides, marriage seemed to have been left be-hind, left outside the colony, as a possibility for people. Even in the ordinance-strangled world before A-Day, folks'd managed to have romances without government permission. But romance, like every-thing else, was on hold here. By unspoken consent it had disappeared from their lives. You took your hun-gers to an amity room and got rid of them there, but marrying and divorcing and all? Too much upset to the balance of life. When nature took its course— because *nothing*, on earth or beneath it, would ever stop women from bearing babies—folks turned a dim eye on the loose morals, and fathers remained largely anonymous.

But he didn't want that.

He wanted secrecy with Ella, sure, and privacy; he didn't fancy making out with her in the middle of the gallery at noontime. He just hoped that folks would gossip about them, would know, somehow, that they were capable of commitment and strong passion. Which was why he was here again tonight, to encourage her to break out again and go up to the piano in the North Reaches. Anything to tie them together, anything to make her realize her need for him.

He watched her stand and begin to clear the table. She wore a skirt tonight, a deep corduroy skirt with red stitching at the hem. Most likely a hand-me-down from some woman who couldn't or wouldn't wear it anymore; Mart didn't recognize it. Ella looked splendid to him, even with her blue utility blouse patched and stained and washed to a limpness. She was in the middle of making a complaint that she had nothing to tell for Episode that night when the sound of someone in the entry caused her to turn, and she dropped five dishes on the floor and said, "Sorb!"

Mart's heart made an ugly contortion in his chest.

Before he even turned to see Sorb, to register with his own eyes the spectacle that was drawing the whole group of Jefferson residents from the table, he felt a colossal echo in the air, a wide wide space on either side of the sound of Ella's voice saying "Sorb!" It was the damned sound of devotion. It was the sound of fancy emotions funneling themselves through the keyhole of a single word, exploding in naked obviousness in the air in the room.

He hated Sorb.

Then he turned. The hate instantly spit itself into a flame and wasted itself away, because Sorb was run mercilessly empty. His face was blue and his eyebrows arched, and the corners of his mouth were brown with dried crud. His hands held his elbows, so his torso was framed square by his arms, and his head tilted a tiny bit forward as if a screw had come loose in his neck. His shiny dark Asian hair was pushed back; sweat or something watered his brow.

"God almighty," said Mem Dora, jumping out of her chair. "Get him to bed."

"It's the lisopress," said Mem Lotus. "He's been through the lisopress. They should've let us know! How dare they send him back on his own."

"Oh, dear," said Mem Troy, trying to concentrate. "Sorb doesn't look like himself."

"Elder Saint Gabriel, how could you?" said Mem Nazira. "Did Sorb go up before the Council? Why didn't you say?"

"I knew nothing—never heard a breath of concern about Sorb—" said Elder Saint Gabriel.

Ella reached him first. She threw her arms around his shoulders. "Come on, quickly, to bed," she said to him, softly, but just at that moment there was silence in the room. Mart heard the naturalness of her words, and the sexy double meaning possible in them. He was sore with the awareness of thinking such a thought at such a time—he couldn't help it, he just couldn't.

Elder Saint Gabriel and Mon Troy pushed quickly into Sorb's cubicle and turned down his sheet and blankets. Even Mem Dora had stopped being aloof and was helping. Mem Troy fluttered around and asked repeatedly if tea and larmer was the right thing, or would it make him vomit? Ella relinquished her hold on Sorb at his doorway, and the older ones took him inside, closed the door, undressed him, and put him to bed. Margaret spent those moments standing between Mart's knees. He had stayed seated at the table, paralyzed by the complexity of his feelings. "It's all right, it's all right, he'll be all right," he told Margaret, and put his arms around her. She stood rigidly.

"Why do they do that?" said Margaret. She didn't turn and face Mart, but looked at the closed door of Sorb's cubicle. "Why does he look like that? What's the matter?"

"I don't know. It's okay, though. He's going to be all right."

"I don't know." Margaret was a serious child; she drove Mart crazy sometimes. "You can hardly tell." She pulled out of Mart's grasp, and went and sat down at the other end of the table where her bowl was set. She addressed the brown pasty gravy in her spoon in a determined but small voice that Mart could only barely hear. "They better not try that on *me.*"

Later, there was tea and larmer made, and lowered voices. Ella's turn at Episode was forgotten for a while. She pulled her chair forward into the adults' circle of chairs, and Mart sat next to her, but back a bit. This wasn't his compound, and Sorb, though a friend, wasn't his first concern.

Still, the memory of his C-Day conversation with

Ella burned in his stomach like an acid soup. She had said to him, "What if you become the next Garner Jones?" or something like that—but here it was Sorb instead. Sorb, who'd never hurt a flea.

Rumor described the lisopress as a kind of electro-chemical bath. Some chemically engineered virus first went through the body and inflamed certain nerves, and then a low-voltage push created a permanent change. At least it was assumed to be permanent; the lisopress was still a recent-enough invention so that it wasn't known to be reversible. Result: mild form of character arrest, personality adjustment. Except in the case of Garner Jones, whose drastic reaction to the treatment had resulted in death—which, of course, no one pretended was reversible.

But why Sorb? It was the Council of Elders that was responsible for deciding on such a therapy. If the Council wasn't formally convened, then the members who were on duty could make the decision. Such had happened with Sorb, apparently—Elder Saint Gabriel swore he knew nothing about the reason. But he promised to find out.

It was hard for Mart—or anyone in Jefferson Compound—to imagine a violation against the government by gentle Sorb Vavilys. True, he was a boy of vivid ideas and quirky courage—but he was also industrious, soft-spoken, pacific by nature. He'd been framed? He'd been the butt of someone's bullying? He'd been caught in a political cross fire? Or had he been stealing, maybe? Mon Troy reminded them all that given the impressionable nature of kids, any doe-eyed slob could turn into a treasonous terrorist. . . .

Ella didn't speak much. Mart watched her being silent. He could only guess that seeing Sorb wasted like this would put the final seal on her refusal to sneak out of drylock and head for the piano. She would resist on the grounds of seeing firsthand the effects of the lisopress treatment. And his craftiness, evasiveness, and charm wouldn't sway her.

It made him feel cold, and determined. He wouldn't let her use this as a tool against him, against their journeys north, he just wouldn't.

When the first curfew tone was sounded, Ella got up and said, "I'll walk you out to the gallery, Mart," and the adults barely noticed them leave. Sorb had been from a good family—no, his family had been cheating and miserable—that was how the conversation was going. Only Elder Saint Gabriel and Mem Dora were silent.

In the corridor, Ella didn't respond to the press of his hand around her waist, or to his mouth biting the air near her right ear. She twitched her head irritably and said, "Cut it out, Mart," and didn't answer his questions until they stood at the entrance to the gallery, when she shook him off and said, "Well, for God's sake, Mart, how can you go on and on like that when Sorb has been brutalized before our very eyes?"

"He'll be all right," said Mart. "You're just taking it too hard."

"Oh, sure," said Ella. "He'll be sick for three or four days and then he'll be fine? Don't be so innocent, Mart—what if he's not? Sometimes it takes a longer recuperation period—it hits some people harder, you know. Remember Garner Jones. And even so, that's not the point. The point is he's in there plowed up with chemical impressions and you stand there like it's just a joke. Aren't you mad about it? He's your friend too, you know."

Mart stuffed his hands in his pockets. Ella the Viking Warrior. "Well, we don't all show our feelings in the same way, Ella. You don't have to question how I feel about Sorb. Sure I'm sorry this happened, but he probably deserved it—"

"What the dickens are you talking about? He deserved it? How can you be so callous?"

He'd made a wrong move. He tried to backtrack. "Well, you don't know what Sorb is up to during the day. Your assignments aren't the same as his. He could be doing just as wrong a thing as we do when we go north to the piano—"

"What he does isn't the point. It's what he deserves—you said he deserved it. He doesn't deserve anything like this. Nobody does. We wouldn't either, if we got caught. You've got rocks in your head sometimes, Mart."

"Don't be so snagging righteous, Ella—it doesn't suit you."

She said, "I'll decide what suits me or not. You can keep your opinions to yourself." She turned and didn't give him a good-night kiss—didn't even offer herself to him for a hug. He was left to walk the rest of the way alone.

Callous? Him?

Callousness turned things sour. It touched good things, fragile things, and twisted them into mawkish, empty things. Sometimes he *did* laugh behind his hand at old women doing their daily prayer thing with the beads and the gestures, or the young men from Carnegie Compound who got down on their knees every morning, wailing out incantations in a garbled ribbon of sound.

But about Sorb? Sorb was a friendly, irritating constant in his life, a man's best friend, like the dog Mart used to have before the poachers shot him for food. Always at the heel, sniffing and bumping and never offended at sharp words or at being forgotten from time to time. Always willing to jump up affectionately and slobber him with unconditional attention and devotion.

Nothing wrong with Sorb that a week's rest wouldn't cure.

Wouldn't it?

12/ Mem Dora

It was a good two days before Sorb was really able to take nourishment, and Ella rearranged her schedule at the glass garden to be able to spend afternoons at home in the compound taking care of him. He was incapable, for a while, of keeping the simplest things down, unless they were spooned into his mouth in very small amounts. So Ella worked at making batches of soup for him every couple of hours, in tiny portions. He smelled terrible, although the men had washed him down several times with warm water and disinfectant. Language was slow coming back to him, but he began with *No*, and then *Thanks*, and she felt like a mother watching a child learn to talk.

After an afternoon nap on the third day, and before the other members of the compound returned home from their daily assignments, Sorb came to a consciousness almost like himself. Ella arrived at the door of his cubicle in delight, with the latest bowlful of saltmash soup. "You called me," she said. "You're feeling better."

"I'm feeling enough to know how terrible I feel," he said. "What day is it?"

She told him. She sat down on the side of his bed with the tray and said, "Sit up and I'll feed you."

"I can feed myself now," he said, but it wasn't true. He tried, and dribbled the soup all over the bedclothes. So Ella dabbed them dry with a towel, fed him, and then didn't want to let him go to sleep again. "Tell me what happened, first, before you have to tell all the others," she said. "I know it'll be different when you tell the others."

At first he didn't speak.

Ella tried to disguise the horror in her system, tried to keep from being rattled with shivers of ice in her blood. Sorb's strange beauty had been forced out of him; he looked waxy and vacant as a child's plastic doll. On the other side of her horror leaned her love for Sorb. Which didn't know what to do with itself. Which wasn't anything like the transforming blaze Mart provoked in her. Which wasn't anything like anything, and now not even like *itself*, because its object—Sorb—wasn't like *him*self anymore.

"Nothing happened," said Sorb at last. "There's nothing to tell."

"Yeah, that's what Elder Saint Gabriel said when he went to the Council of Elders. Couldn't get an answer from them, or so he said." She put her hands in her lap and waited.

So he told her, in phrases which were at first poorly

87

locked together, but which, as he grew stronger, made better sense. He was vague for a while, and bits and pieces were missing. Mem Dora as a political dissenter? *That* was hard to swallow. Ella wondered if he was making some of this up. A memory, a conversation, a plan, a dream: What was real, what was in his imagination?

"They killed the angel," he said, sitting up suddenly in bed. "Like Garner Jones, they killed the angel and shoved it in the chiller. You know why, Ella, you know why?"

"Shhh," said Ella, "calm down. I should've waited, I guess—"

" 'Cause they don't want us to burn the place down," said Sorb. "We burn so hard we'll melt this ice maze—they don't want that, Ella, they don't." He leaned forward, his eyes rolled inward, and he vomited suddenly, thin milk, into his lap.

That evening, Mart came by the compound for the first time since the night Sorb had staggered in, bruised and inchoate. Mart gave big smiles to everyone there except Ella; he avoided her, he didn't even pass a look her way. Mem Lotus leaped up and said, "Your friend is better, Mart—he's ready to see you. Come on now and his heart will jump up." She took Mart by the hand as if he were four years old, and walked him over to Sorb's cubicle. "Look who's come to see you now that you're better, Sorb, your own Mart."

Ella, sitting in the rocking chair, felt her insides

twist against each other like two fists in one glove. Ruination and rue. With Sorb so sick, she needed Mart's companionship. But he was getting back at her for being snappy the other night. Her teeth bit down on her inner lip. Drew blood.

She turned her chair so she couldn't see the door of Sorb's cubicle, but she heard the door shut tightly behind Mart. "Margaret, do you want me to tell you a story?" she said brightly, but Margaret was busy playing with Andrew and wouldn't be distracted. "Mem Lotus, let me help you shred the acemyte for tomorrow," she said, but Mem Lotus shooed her away. "You've been working hard all day," said Ella in protest, but Mem Lotus declared everlasting fondness for work and she wanted to do it herself.

Then, short of going out for a walk, there was nothing else to do. The Troys were playing cards, Mem Waterhouse was reading her Bible. Elder Saint Gabriel was out visiting some other compound, and Mon Gorky and Mem Nazira were trying to speak to each other in some foreign language that neither of them could remember very well, and laughing hysterically. Mem Dora was repairing a skirt of Margaret's with a needle and thread, snipping patches from the hem allowance and stitching them onto worn spots here and there. Ella sat down next to her and watched.

A glamorous woman sewing sewed differently than anyone else. The arch of the wrist, the angle of the head. Beauty and self-possession churned out of Mem Dora like warmth from a heating coil. Maybe it was Sorb's strange suggestion that Mem Dora had been a political activist. That possibility of humanness made Ella lean forward and say, "I wonder if you know more about love than anyone else here."

"You have something on your mind?" said Mem Dora sharply.

All about Mart, his smug brightness. All about Sorb and his darker power. Fear, and love, and fear of love. "I just wonder, how's someone like me to learn anything about love if people like you never say anything about your own life? At Episode you only tell stories from books you read, never anything that really happened—"

"A private life is still possible no matter who makes the rules," said Mem Dora, looking up, eyes solemn and focused on Ella for a short time. "You can wonder all you like but I'm not obliged to answer your questions."

"I know you're not obliged," said Ella, rather angry at her suddenly, and knowing she was really being angry at Mart for ignoring her. "I just said we're curious. I thought a human question might bring a human response. I forgot I was talking to a *star*. I see I was wrong. Excuse *me*."

"Don't be so irritable," said Mem Dora, not getting angry, just attending to her work. "We've had everything taken from us, everything. We're people whose pasts have been stolen from us—we can't verify them, we can't even be sure if what we remember is real. That goes for 'stars' as well as for everyone else. I believe strongly in Episode—it was the only stroke of intelligence shown when we first came here to

Pioneer Colony. But my own past is my own, and if I gave it away I'd have nothing left at all."

"You have Margaret," said Ella.

"Margaret isn't mine," said Mem Dora.

Ella stared. Mem Dora said quickly, "I don't mean she's not my child. I mean that she doesn't belong to me. She's her own self, is Margaret, and she'll have her own world, if we survive this entombment. Margaret will give herself to anyone or to no one, as she likes; but I can't be greedy and keep her for myself."

Such a hard face on such a beautiful woman, thought Ella, looking cautiously, as if for the first time. Mem Dora had her short hair in a kerchief, blue with gold squares, and her downcast eyes were brown and strong, sunk in a face whose skin had tightened to show the high cheekbones, the firm jaw. Her skin was a glossier, lighter color than that of other people of Haitian descent who lived in the colony. Mem Dora was as small as a teenager, with her sapling-thin waist, narrow wrists, dainty ankles swallowed up by thermostockings. How had she looked on the stage? Ella had been too young to pay attention to things like that, back in the life above ground.

Mem Dora was easy to dislike. She was so stubborn and righteous and silent, and self-effacing to the point of being exclusive. Even now, jabbing the needle in and out of the skirt, she projected a silent defiance of the whole compound. Why was Ella liking her nonetheless?

"You've got to give me something," said Ella suddenly. "It's one thing for you to be distant from the adults, because they know how to take it. But *I've* never done anything to you. Have I?"

"What do you want?"

Ella thought of Mart in there talking to Sorb. What she really wanted was to know how to love someone, how much was right, how much was wrong. She wanted to know how to keep from being jealous of Mart and Sorb's friendship, which was stronger, she knew, than Mart ever acknowledged. She wanted to know how to be able to love Mart without letting him rule her as if she were a planet to be subdued, a shell to be smashed open. But she couldn't say any of these things to Mem Dora. She could barely say them inside her own head, to herself.

"You won't sing, ever, will you?" she said sadly. "What I really want is to hear you sing."

"I won't do that for you, Ella Mencken," said Mem Dora. "I've given my word to myself. It's just battering yourself to even ask me."

"But why not?"

Mem Dora didn't speak.

"I want to hear music," said Ella. "I want to make it." Free of obligation to Mart, she thought.

Mem Dora broke the thread and knotted it, stuck the needle back in the sewing kit. "You used to play the piano, didn't you?" she said. "But with the inspired planning by government committee, you have no piano to play on. They didn't get flutes and violins and clarinets in here on time. Just a big truckload of electrical equipment that has been dead for two years. Just as they didn't manage to get decent paint-

92

ings in these phony windows, just those postcard views of questionable interest."

There *is* a piano in the colony, Ella wanted to say. But it's a secret—in storage as if it's a dangerous weapon.

The door behind Ella was opening. A wreath of laughter was escaping from Sorb's cubicle. Mart would be coming out. He'd either come over and try to get into her good graces for having done the compassion routine and been to visit the sick, or he'd be ignoring her still, out of spite. She missed Mart, she wanted his attention. Not his domination. "I used to play the piano," she said, "but how can I, now?"

Mem Dora turned her eyes to Ella, as Mart was leaving Sorb's cubicle with noisy friendliness. "I won't sing for you because I won't sing for anyone," she said quietly, "but we will find a place to go, and I'll teach you to sing for yourself."

Then she snapped back inside of herself and kept on sewing.

13/ The Music Lesson

Settled in an amity room, they looked at each other briefly. Mem Dora had a no-nonsense expression on her face that made Ella nervous; she began to be sorry she'd spoken to her last week. Could singing be taught by such a stony face? How much of learning depends on trusting, thought Ella—would she be able to trust Mem Dora?

The beginning wasn't good. Ella, trying to put Mem Dora at ease, asked conversationally when had Mem Dora begun her singing career? And Mem Dora had answered, "Sing me an F sharp above middle C."

So conversation was forbidden. Ella blushed as if she'd been slapped, and moved backward a bit—though in the cramped quarters of an amity room there wasn't much space for retreating. She searched in the well of her musical mind for a middle C. Found it, hummed it to herself, climbed up the scale four notes and sharped it. Sang it as defiantly as possible.

"You're flat," said Mem Dora, "by almost a half step. Sharp it."

Ella shoved it up a hair.

"There, that's it. You've got the note now even if your quality is poor. Come down an octave."

Ella thought it out, then dropped the note in a glissando curve.

"You'll learn not to hesitate," said Mem Dora in a bored way, as if she'd been teaching girls to sing for a decade. "An octave, an eleventh, a sixth will become as natural to your voice as the extension was natural to your hand in playing octaves on the keyboard. Now let's find your range."

Ella sang down, and then, in half steps, up two octaves and some. When she finished there was a pained silence for a moment.

"You've thought, I guess," said Mem Dora, "about joining that choir that Mem Strickney up in Dickinson directs? I don't know why you shouldn't enjoy that. There's plenty of young people there—"

Ella cautiously explained. "I went when I was younger. They're so sloppy. She doesn't really know what she's doing, and the adults laugh at her behind her back, and the kids fool around and don't try. They sing all that stuff like 'Peace Comes Once a Year' and 'Brightly Burning.' I don't want to make fun of music. I want it to be serious."

Mem Dora said, "Well, you should know what you want. But I'm surprised you don't seem to be very interested in other people your age. Except Mart and Sorb. You would meet other kids there. You don't have many friends, do you—?"

"Is that important to my learning how to sing?" said Ella coolly, and then, in a more normal tone, "Besides, lots of the kids there aren't my age. Or else they're creeps or something. Besides, it's not really the point, is it? Having friends?"

"Not really," said Mem Dora. "Tell me what you remember of your parents."

"Are you out of your mind?"

"No."

"My parents disappeared when I was six—years before the Colony closed its doors."

"Do you know why?"

"No, I don't," said Ella. "They left me with my uncle. And he committed larceny to get me the proper datacard to get here, and he was frazzled for it. As far as I know, they're both dead, my parents. Like everybody else."

"Yes, they are."

Ella wondered why she wasn't knocked speechless. "You knew them? And for four years or so we've been holed up in the same compound and you never mentioned it before? What's the matter with you anyway? How did you know them?"

Mem Dora had a look of bitter reluctance on her face—the same look her daughter Margaret displayed at medicine time. Set, regretful, with a granite kind of imperviousness—but not closed. No, there was a lot there, open to the observing eye. Ella watched carefully.

"We met in Paris," said Mem Dora, "when I was young. Just starting out. Transcontinental travel was much more popular—and possible—then. The governments hadn't yet begun their fiscal regulations and quota wars. I had a job singing in the Café Jardin on Boulevard Saint Germaine. Lead singer with Mem Ruby Prendergast and her band."

What a phrase, what a thought. The exotic sound of it even seemed to catch Mem Dora up short; she took a moment to study her work-bruised nails and flex her fingers before going on.

"One night at the Café Jardin—a particularly busy night; we'd just had a rave notice on the satellite report—Mem Prendergast came up to me and told me that two good friends of hers were in town and coming by, and would I sing a song directly to their table? It was your parents, Ella—Mem and Mon Mencken. Mem Prendergast had known them in the so-called Music Embargo of 'Seventeen. So I agreed. Trotted out my best number at the time, an old song from way back—'Glory Orbit'—and gave it its brightest treatment.

"Your folks were young then, as I was young, but already they had had their life work cut out for them, busy in the chemical peace movement. I hadn't heard of that, or of any of the other resistances going on in Europe and America and Asia—so your parents meant nothing to me except as friends of Mem Ruby's. And I wouldn't remember another fact about that evening except that they hadn't come to the Café Jardin alone. They brought with them their friend Mon John Prite, who was then a young law student, in Paris with his father on business. So that was where I met the man who would be my husband, sitting at the table with your parents."

"Well, how do you know my parents are dead?"

"The chemical peace movement, Ella, don't you know anything about it?"

Ella shook her head.

"The Wash-heads decimated it before your time—"

"Wash-heads?"

"Government agents from Washington. Wash-heads—implying, to the Left at least, a kind of thoughtless brainwashed allegiance to official government policy."

"Then it's true—you were an activist!"

Mem Dora threw back her head and laughed. "I were indeed."

"So what happened?"

"So the Wash-heads shredded the chemical peace movement from inside out. They infiltrated its ranks, somehow, and it fell apart in miserable pieces. I heard corroborating stories from a number of different people that your parents died in an early-morning raid. Your parents were powerful people, Ella—not powerful as John was, in public, nor as I was even, despite myself—but behind the scene: really. They moved people, they got things done. You can be proud of them. They believed in an America described all those years ago in the Declaration of Independence—and they believed at a time when most people had stopped believing in anything."

"Did you know them well?"

"We never met again," said Mem Dora, "but I heard about them through my husband. I know one thing for sure: It was for your own good that they gave you over to your uncle for raising. They thought they would be targets for a government wipe-out campaign—and, of course, they were right. They saved you from that."

Ella said, "Tell me more."

"There's nothing more to tell. I only told you this much because you accused me the other evening of being close-mouthed. And I thought it over, and decided that while I have every right to husband my own memories about my own past, what I know of *your* past could rightly be said to belong to you. So now I've given it to you, with apologies if I've caused you any distress by waiting this long. You just didn't seem old enough before."

"So I just turned old enough, just like that?"

"You asked me about love," said Mem Dora, and for once there was a smile on her face. It came there so suddenly that Ella was dazzled out of all proportion by it. It was like what she remembered of fireworks—noise and stars and surprise, all at once drawing an "Oh!" from deep inside. But like fireworks, the smile faded, and Mem Dora said softly, "If you can love someone, you can learn how to act." She resumed her usual self-satisfied composure. "Now: Let's talk about pitch."

"We were talking about the Dead," said Ella. "It's all too fast. How can I take all this in and think about pitch?"

"Make your choice," said Mem Dora. "It's that or nothing. Don't waste my time."

The rest of the hour ran by then like water. Breathing, tone, pitch, arpeggios, exercises, shaping of vowels, enunciating of consonants, extension of lungs, firmness of jaw, strength of spine. Ella itched to take notes, but Mem Dora wouldn't let her. You have to know this all inside yourself, you can't review it by reading notes, she said. Ella didn't do a lot of singing, and Mem Dora didn't do any. But by the time they both rose to go back to the compound, Ella felt swamped and damp with the sound of singing, hungry, thirsty, and satisfied all at the same time.

She wanted to tell Sorb everything she'd learned about Mem Dora, and about her own parents, but Sorb, bad luck, was reading in his cubicle until dinner. At the table, he sat down with Margaret Prite on his lap, so there wasn't any way to bring it up then. And in the hour between dinner and Episode, he disappeared. Off to see Mart in Lincoln Compound.

After a couple of minutes of full-strength frustration, she strode out of Jefferson Compound. She didn't care if she was still angry at Mart for being so casual about Sorb's lisopress treatment. Mart had been giving Sorb a good deal of attention in the past week— in part to prove her wrong, no doubt, in part to snub her—and she wasn't going to put up with it anymore. Sorb should have asked her along. Nothing got better unless you worked to make it so. It was the nature of things like this to stay the same or get worse.

100

What was she thinking, why was she so agitated? She was striding along like a lunatic. She could feel herself sweating on her neck, under her curly hair, and at her temples.

As she strode, a living breathing being, through the maze of these metal cells, harboring people like a large though claustrophobic beehive, she was somehow—but how to say it?—a fuller person. Fuller for knowing that her parents were indeed dead—and dead not by the menace that had chased residents into the Pioneer Colony, but dead as a result of their convictions and behavior. Almost dead by choice instead of by chance, and in some perverse way she felt proud of that.

Relieved by it.

Challenged? Positively challenged! She wanted to talk about it against all rules, to blast it from the third floor of the gallery. My parents were *real*.

Sorb would appreciate this, even lioopressed Sorb. He liked action, courage. It would be like a course of adrenalin to him, in this state, to hear the story of her agitating parents.

But she couldn't find him. Agnes Treasure, the nine-year-old monster who terrorized Margaret Prite in the grammar room, told Ella when she arrived at Lincoln Compound that Sorb had come by and gone away again, with Mart. She didn't know where they'd gone, and even if she did, she wouldn't tell.

"Thank you, Agnes Treasure," said Ella with exaggerated politeness. "You are always such a treat to talk to."

"I know," said Agnes. "Tell me something new."
Ella resisted temptation.

The gallery was busy with people having after-dinner conversations. Ella scanned it quickly. She then walked up to the amity rooms and tried the door of the room in which she and Mem Dora had practiced, but a voice said, "Private meeting in progress," and she knew what *that* meant. She didn't want to visit compound by compound, and she didn't think it necessary anyway. One thing that she and Sorb and Mart had always had in common was a distance from the other kids. It wasn't likely that Sorb and Mart would have suddenly struck up new friendships.

Climbing the stairs to the Utility Belt, she passed Mon Conway, the j-guard, and almost asked him if he'd seen Sorb and Mart on his rounds, but she thought better of it. If Mart had taken Sorb up to the piano, up in the North Reaches, Ella didn't want to be the one to jeopardize their excursion.

But in all the places she could think to look, and not be in danger of breaking any rules, Sorb and Mart were absent. So she gave up eventually—it was nearing Episode anyway—and returned to Jefferson.

It was Elder Saint Gabriel's night for Episode.

But tonight Ella couldn't hear him. She could only think of Mem Dora. Being unable to share the loud and astounding news of her parents, her mind had shrunk from that story. There was only the living left: Mem Dora. As a young woman, singing in a café in Paris, France. Ella closed her eyes as if concentrating on Elder Saint Gabriel's monotone.

She saw in her mind a room, painted deep red, like the red she remembered when she thought of roses.

Mediterranean palms in large ceramic pots here and there among the tables.

No good picture of Mem Ruby Prendergast and her orchestra, so Ella thought of them behind a folding screen made of acemyte paper, on which were painted delicate sprigs of lilac and wild cornflower. "And now, the Café Jardin is proud to present a new talent: the Morning Star herself: Mem Dora Prite!" Only of course if she hadn't yet met Mon John Prite her name would have been different.

Anyway: Here she comes. Dressed in a tight white dress with a low bodice. Pearls. This would be an old-fashioned place, with a hand microphone instrument, not a laser-tracked electronic mike trained to hover just above her mouth. She would come out and smile. Applause! Mem Ruby Prendergast's band would begin with something perky.

She would open her mouth after the thirty-two bar introduction, she would smile as she had smiled this afternoon, with a broad mouth full of perfect teeth, and she would belt out the first note—

But this was where the fantasy went wrong, because Ella had no imagination about how Mem Dora Prite handled a song. She couldn't remember it from her childhood, she didn't have it as part of her current memory. In her mind, Mem Dora was standing on the top step, ready to blast up the room with the dynamite of her voice, but she could never get started, and Mem Ruby Prendergast's band just held the note out. . . .

Then Ella realized that the curfew tone had sounded, and Elder Saint Gabriel, to everyone's relief, was saying, "Well, that'll have to be that, folks."

She cleaned her teeth, tried to clean her thoughts of Mem Dora Prite, and only as she laid herself down on her bed did she realize that Sorb still had not returned.

14/ Pot on the Boil

There were two filaments burning inside her: fury and fear. They burned with alternating brilliance as she stood in the common area watching the adults puzzle and argue. Sorb's cubicle was empty at dawn: Should they report it, should they let it go? If he'd gotten himself in trouble somewhere and didn't show up for assignment, the absence would be recorded, and Sorb'd be in even worse trouble than he'd been before.

Mon Draper, the teacher, alerted the j-guards that Sorb and Mart were missing from class. The news spread like the plague.

As far as Ella could see, the pot had been brought to the boil. She could not remember Pioneer ever more riled up than this, since the early days when self-governance with the system of the Council of Elders was invented and locked into place. The measure of an event's importance could be taken by the number of colonists who were discussing it, and this event was top value for gossip.

Ella listened, as she walked home, to the tones of voice rather than the actual words she was hearing. In the voices: anger, contempt, surprise, foreboding, dismay. She didn't hear encouragement or sympathy, delight or anything else. Even Agnes Treasure, jumping rope in an exercise court, was chanting, "Two, four, six, eight, jolt them quick 'cause we can't wait." A bevy of grinning kids was clustered around her.

"Margaret, get over here," said Ella sharply, when she saw Margaret Prite hanging around the edges of the crowd. "You should know better than that," she scolded as they headed for Jefferson.

But Margaret didn't know better. No one seemed to know better.

In the common area of Jefferson Compound stood Sorb and Mart, at last. Filthy as the dead-and-buried, a circle of dust on the floor around them. The Troys, Mem Waterhouse, and Mem Dora arranged there, gawking.

Margaret cried out and ran toward Sorb, but the electricity of argument stopped her halfway there, and she turned and went to her mother's side instead.

"The lie seeks out the liar, and becomes a worm in his soul," said Mem Waterhouse. "Part and parcel of a lie I won't be."

"Jesus Buddha Krishna Christ," exploded Mart, "I'm not asking you to lie. Just don't say anything if you don't want to say anything, is all."

106

"What's going on?" cried Ella, ashamed of breaking in and taking the attention but having to know.

"You stay out of this—it's too much already," said Mon Troy.

"Honey, what's going on?" asked his befuddled wife.

"We'll be frazzled," said Mart simply. "We've been ducking and hiding and slipping by for hours just to get back here undetected. If you don't alibi us, we'll be juiced to the nines. Ella, tell them. We were here last night, weren't we?"

Mem Dora spoke up. She so seldom took part in the daily dilemmas that everyone stood open-mouthed while she rattled off her ideas. "You boys get down to the shower room, quick, and clean off that dust and dirt. It's more incriminating than a thousand alibis could hide. Here's a story: You boys were both with me last night in my cubicle. It's nobody's business but ours what we were doing there. If the j-guards get you before you get back here, those are the facts. You got here before supper last night. I didn't mention your presence, and nobody has asked me yet. Got that? Good luck. Now go on!"

"Come on, help us out," said Mart, grabbing Sorb's hand as he looked around at Mem Troy, Mon Troy, and Mem Waterhouse. "We won't survive a juicing. This one especially." And he ran off, past Ella without looking at her, dragging Sorb. The smell of the dust on their tunics was rare, foul, and special. Ella sniffed its awfulness with joy, since conversation wasn't possible.

"This is wrong, Mem Dora," said Mem Waterhouse lethally. "It's scandal. Crime and abomination. You're standing there with a child on your hip and you're going to claim that you entertained two youths in your cubicle overnight, in her presence?"

"She sleeps soundly, Margaret does, don't you, dear?" said Mem Dora after a time.

Mem Troy's mouth opened and closed several times.

"But where were they?" said Ella. "How long have they been back?"

"Off out of drylock, apparently," said Mon Troy. "Mem Dora, I appreciate your warm feelings for the boys, but your feelings are misguided. You have a reputation to maintain—if not for yourself, then for your child. Think of her."

"Sorb hasn't done so well in the lisopress, Mon Troy," said Mem Dora. "Or haven't you noticed? He's a little off kilter. Taken it harder than some would. He's the one likely to be damaged again now, not Margaret. And Mart—if Mart is that clever that he can break the drylock—well, we need him whole and entire, Mon Troy. He's of value to all of us. Margaret knows who I am—or she will, sooner or later. If she can't learn, that's her problem."

"I can so learn, Mommy," said Margaret, somewhat sullenly.

"It's not a question of complicity in a crime," said Mem Dora. "It's a question, Mem Waterhouse, of protecting these two boys from permanent damage."

"The whole of Jefferson will be implicated," said Mem Waterhouse.

The argument continued until a clatter of footsteps sounded in the hallway. Moving much more rapidly than usual, Mem Lotus came into the compound. "Mercy, the dust, sweep it up," she said, "we're about to have company—the j-guards, besides! I averted my eyes once I saw who they had—the j-guards have hauled Sorb and Mart stark naked out of the showers, glistening like acemyte and dripping all over the floors, up through the gallery. Oh, the fuss, and the humiliation for them! And someone told me the j-guards were on their way here next—to interrogate. Mem Troy, please, the broom, we can't have this mess. What's the bad smell?"

"Mem Waterhouse," said Mem Dora, "and Mon Troy and Mem Troy, you didn't hear a word of what was said earlier. You either, Ella. There can't be another solution than the one I've proposed."

"Are you threatening me?" said Mem Waterhouse. "Is that a threat?"

"No, of course not," said Mem Dora, smiling broadly as footsteps sounded again in the corridor. "What kind of a woman would do such a thing as that?"

15/ The Hearing

What they'd endured!

And now this!

They were kept dancing through the metallic halls and walkways, spattering drops of water onto the astounded colonists. Mon Micklersohn, Mon Conway, and some newly enlisted j-guard ushered them along, with Elder Johnson, who averted his eyes from their giddy illegal nakedness.

Their clean clear nakedness, all traces of dust washed away.

They'd soaped and scrubbed, gasping in their hurry, snorting on swallowed water, using much more water than their ration. Every patch of skin cleansed was a disguise. "Your legs, the calves," Sorb had warned, "and how's my back? Do my back! And your hair's gone brown with dirt—rinse it again!" They'd grinned like four year olds. Sorb had splashed Mon Conway in the face when he'd first charged through the steaming mist to grab him.

Mart was bristling with defiance, anger, so enraged that he could hardly keep from leaping around onto old grisly Mon Micklersohn, who had his two hands fastened like mebber clamps onto Mart's biceps—Mart's arms were twisted behind his back, and his sterling clean hands were cuffed together with burglar's horrors. Mon Conway and the other j-guard hadn't embarrassed Sorb with burglar's horrors, but walked arm in arm with him, their uniforms damp with the contact.

Sorb's head was bowed, but his smile was broad. He was apparently unaware of the spectacle he was making, so great was his relief at having an alibi. "Afternoon, Mem Mbulu," he called, "how are you doing?"

Colonists stared, whispered, looked away and back again. Public nakedness, Mart knew, was almost a proof of guilt in itself: Even if he and Sorb managed to weather the storm of accusations about breaking drylock, they would be forever branded as having been lewd in the corridors of Pioneer Colony—no matter that they were being marched along by respectable officers of the law. It was the ultimate humiliation. Only Mart, astounded by himself, could barely identify any humiliation in his own reactions to the crisis. Just quenchless rage.

At Control, he and Sorb were thrown into a room with a bench and a couple of eye-jolting rig-ups, which he hoped wouldn't need to be used. Outside, someone scrambled for towels and a couple of robes. Finally Elder Johnson came in, leaving the door wide open and the j-guards righteously sullen in the antechamber.

"Dry up, boys," said Elder Johnson calmly. "Seems to me you've got a long evening ahead of you and you might as well be dry."

"We didn't do a thing, honest," said Sorb, shivering.

"Don't waste your breath. We'll get your Elders in here and go through things molecule by molecule if need be."

Mart slung the towel quickly around his waist. There, that much was set to rights.

"Dry my back, Mart," said Sorb.

"None of that," said Elder Johnson.

"I'd like him to *dry* my *back*," said Sorb with unusual deliberateness. "Do you mind?"

Elder Johnson withdrew.

As they waited, fidgeting, for the Elders to convene, they couldn't talk, discuss their alibi, offer each other courage, congratulate each other on wild luck gone full-moon full so far. J-guards would report any word. So they sat on the bench, touching shoulders, an imperishable hope kept on simmer.

Mart felt *fiery* with hope. Hope so wide-ranging that he hardly knew what deserved the credit for it. He'd done so many dangerous things before, without detection, it seemed natural to suppose he'd be caught one day soon. He was glad it wasn't on an excursion with Ella; he'd have felt somehow more responsible than with Sorb. Well, it was Sorb's fault that they were caught anyway. And maybe they'd slip through the charges.

"You scared?" said Sorb.

112

"Shut up," he said kindly. "You're just entertaining the troops, you know."

"I don't care," said Sorb. "We've been a barrel of entertainment already today."

The Elders convened in a long shallow room, sitting on one side of a table. Mart knew only a few of them well: Elder Fitchell from his own compound, Elder Saint Gabriel from Jefferson, and Elder Johnson, the president, from Adams. The other ones possessed familiar faces and their names seemed to come and go, like blinking lights. That was how Mart knew that he must be frightened.

Nine solid old-man faces, as if carved on marble: staring, slack-jowled, unsmiling. Four old-woman faces, no less sober. One young man, an officious agent named Elder Moxie-doxie, of all unlikely names.

Elder Johnson called in the captain of the j-guards, who made some official report so congested with citations and jargon that Mart couldn't follow it.

Of course, it'd been twenty-four hours since they'd eaten: That was why Mart couldn't concentrate. And why Sorb was looking dizzy—although Sorb had been so scrubbed inside out from his lisopress treatment that looking dizzy was a permanent state these days. Even now his head was sliding toward Mart's shoulder. "Watch it," Mart muttered. Sorb pulled himself up.

Elder Johnson put the question to them. Did they or did they not break drylock last night and spend the curfew hours in the off-limits Reaches outside the Centrex globe?

"Why, not at all," said Mart.

Sorb looked uncertain. Mart jostled him. "Do you think," said Sorb, unconvincingly dramatic, "that we'd do such an imbecilic thing—?"

"Answer the question," droned Elder Fitchell, a curly-haired witch who had teeth like mingo sticks. She cleared her lips off her expansive teeth, and smiled.

"In a word," said Sorb, "put us down for a resounding *no* on that one."

"Levity won't help. It'll hinder you," said Elder Johnson.

"If we can't have levity," said Sorb, "let's settle for brevity. On with the show."

Mart elbowed him again, and Sorb seemed to come out of his daze. "Excuse me, Elder Johnson, I'm just not used to procedures like this," said Sorb in a voice more like his natural one. "Please don't take offense."

"Whether or not offense is intended," shot Elder Moxie-doxie, "offense is taken!"

"Indeed," said Elder Fitchell, closing her lips over her teeth.

"Well, give it back, I didn't mean for you to have it," said Sorb.

"Mon Vavilys!" said Elder Johnson. "You fail to realize the seriousness of your situation! The charges brought against you and Mon Rengage—and I dignify you with your adult titles in advance of your eighteenth birthdays in order to stress the gravity of your situations—are capable of landing you both with the most strict and unpleasant of punishments. You should—"

"Like Garner Jones?" said Sorb.

There was a silence—because a minor had interrupted an Elder.

"That's an inappropriate remark," said Elder Johnson. "You should know, Mon Vavilys, that what happened to Garner Jones was an accident."

"Who remembers the bones of Garner Jones?" said Sorb.

"Hey, Sorb." Mart tugged at his sleeve. *"Shut up."*

Elder Johnson seemed shaken. He coughed into a tissue and then resumed in a milder voice. "Any punishment will be in keeping with the common code as interpreted by our host of Elders. You'd be well advised to keep your flippancies to yourself, boys. Mart Rengage, you may wish to answer for the two of you. I speak on your behalf in that suggestion."

"Sorb, let me finish," said Mart. Sorb shrugged.

The Elders focused their attention on Mart now. How odd for him to be spokesperson—it was a new and unlikable job. Usually Mart had the hot temper, the thoughtless words, the ability to make folks hostile. Sorb was known to be gentle as a brussels sprout, in love with and loved by everyone. Mart swallowed hard, and resolved to exhibit, instantly, all of the most winning qualities he'd ever seen in Sorb.

So on it went. The same question about the breaking of drylock last night was asked again and again. Since drylock was so well understood by Mart, and since none of the Elders were technicians, Mart found it easy to snow them by misusing the few technical terms they knew and understood. "What do you take me for, a wizard? I ought to be flattered," he hissed at one point, and then resaid it, nicely. "I *am* flattered—Mon Draper in school never gave me such credit for the kind of brains you think I must have."

Then the time came to release the alibi.

"We were in Jefferson last night," said Mart softly.

"That's a lie," said Elder Saint Gabriel. He looked sadly at Mart. "You can't expect me to let that by, Mart."

"You didn't know we were there. What else can you say?" Mart hoped he didn't begin to sweat too obviously at this point.

"I was in Jefferson all night last night, Episode on through morning," said Elder Saint Gabriel. "You weren't there, and Sorb was gone, too. There was a lot of worry about Sorb, especially after his recent lisopress. We conferred quite energetically about it. I'm afraid you'll have no voice to speak on your behalf."

"Well, no one knew we were there."

"Where could you be that no one knew?" Elder Saint Gabriel seemed almost apologetic in the softness of his replies.

"It would be compromising to say," said Mart craftily.

"I will have to insist," said Elder Johnson, but Mart didn't care anymore what happened, for he saw in Elder Saint Gabriel's eyes the sudden intuitive grasp of what the alibi must be, would have to be. A tremendous crackle of anger surfaced for a moment in Elder Saint Gabriel's expression, before it was supplanted by a look of respect, defeat, staggered incredulity. Mart knew in that moment that the alibi would work.

"We spent the night in the cubicle of Mem Dora Prite," he said, fading his voice away on the end of the line so that he sounded mortified, but not so faded that they couldn't recognize every separate, triumphant syllable.

When the meeting was resumed the next day, the Elders looked exhausted. Sorb and Mart sat up smartly in their best tunics and neatly pressed trousers. Mem Dora Prite stood behind them, refusing the seat offered her.

Mart knew better than to be smug. But things were going well. Even during their night in the tiny separate cells—no more than two long slots into which they had to climb, feet first, and lie still, like two corpses in coffins stacked one atop the other—the rumor got back to them that the Elders' questioning of Jefferson residents had gone in their favor. Mon Conway, the j-guard they knew best because he'd once been a student with them, had stood gossiping with them before morning. Confusion at Jefferson, he told them, and a number of residents made firm statements that although the boys *might* have been in Mem Dora's cubicle, they couldn't prove that they *had* been. Or that they hadn't. Elder Saint Gabriel was silent through the whole interrogation process,

117

Mon Conway said. You'd think he had engineered the cover-up himself.

By this Mart realized that there was little doubt among the colonists that it *was* a cover-up—that he and Sorb had in fact broken drylock, trespassed on forbidden Reaches, enlisted the aid of Mem Dora in a scandalous but invincible alibi. He didn't care. It didn't matter what people thought. The antique rituals of justice would preserve him and Sorb. Although he'd dozed through dozens of civics classes, he'd learned at least this much: A person was innocent until proven guilty. Hell, it was inscribed on the old laminium dollar coins underneath the profile of President Shapiro. A tenet of pre-Pioneer days that people held firmly on to even now.

Mem Dora answered Elder Johnson's questions in a curt and businesslike way, no posing or primping, no pouting. She sounded more like a lawyer than a nightclub singer.

"No. I didn't consider public opinion when I invited the boys to my cubicle.

"No. I don't care to discuss our conversations or activities during the night in question.

"Yes. I'm aware that there are rules against inviting guests into one's private cubicle.

"I am not interested in public opinion, Elder Johnson. The public can consider me the Whore of Babylon if it likes. I'm more interested in the statements of individuals—including myself. You, Elder Johnson, might want to tell me what *you* think of a woman who entertains not one but two good-looking underage

118

young men in her private cubicle overnight while her six-year-old daughter sleeps soundly all night long."

Elder Johnson said, "My personal opinion of the matter isn't pertinent to the discussion."

"No more is public opinion, Elder Johnson. There's doing and there's talking. No one can prove seduction or proselytism or any other crime against public morals. Therefore the talking of it has a curious hollow ring to it."

Mart could see astonishment and disapproval on the faces of some of the Elders. But Elder Zink, a woman with crumbling skin and a bald spot right near her crown, leaned forward and said, "We must be just. We must not be rash. Mem Dora isn't so far off the mark about public opinion. We're here to try to determine whether she's telling the truth, not whether she offends our moral sensibilities. Let's keep the questioning, Elder Johnson, on that line."

Elder Johnson nodded curtly, called for more questions.

Mart answered much as Mem Dora had: short, unhelpful, offended answers. No, they wouldn't say why they had spent the night in Mem Dora's cubicle. No, they didn't consider what people might think. Yes, they were aware of the regulations forbidding the breaking of curfew and the visiting of cubicles at night. Yes, they were prepared to accept the consequences.

"Who atones for Garner Jones?" said Sorb, a kind of burp that everyone ignored.

Then Elder Johnson said, "Just one more witness

119

before we break for deliberation. In view of the unusual situation, I've decided to allow the next witness to be questioned in the presence of the whole court. Mon Whalen, please?"

The j-guard opened the door, and in came Margaret Prite, holding tightly to the hand of Ella Mencken.

Oh, Ella, thought Mart, go on back, leave her here alone, you shouldn't be here. Even in the vise grip of the current dilemma, he was fascinated and angry at her, even now. She was being so aloof, and contained, and strong.

She had that way with children that soothed them, and Margaret looked controlled and mature beyond her years. Ella had turned away from him, and gone weak over Sorb when Sorb had been lisopressed; Ella had charged him with brutality of emotion and hollowness of heart. She looked as grand as an animal, standing there just behind Margaret, although Mart couldn't think which animal could look so stirring, smooth, alive, and pained. He wished she would leave.

"You may go to your mother, Margaret," said Elder Johnson kindly.

Margaret wouldn't move.

"I'll just stay here with her. She's frightened," said Ella. "If you could just be quick—"

Mart couldn't see, nor could he imagine, the look on Mem Dora's face when Margaret stood there, unmoving. He could merely sense her body as a rigid force of natural energy held in check behind him.

But he was gratified to hear that the questions put to Margaret were not sly, mean, or intimidating.

What time had she gone to sleep the night before last? Had anyone else been in the cubicle besides her mother? What do you think they were doing there—?

"Inappropriate question," sang out Elder Zink.

Why had she not told Elder Saint Gabriel or some other adult? Didn't she know that visiting cubicles after curfew was against the law?

"Yes. I didn't know that," said Margaret.

What time had they left in the morning?

Where had they slept?

"Beep," said Elder Zink.

"This is a question of ascertaining truth or falsehood, not of leveling accusations of immorality, Elder Zink," said Elder Johnson. "Answer the question, Margaret."

Margaret took a firmer grasp on Ella's hand. "I don't know. I was asleep."

"They didn't sleep in your bed."

"I sleep like a rock," said Margaret, and the Elders laughed, despite themselves. Even Elder Fitchell opened her mouth, and her teeth bit huge gulps of air as she shook.

"I sleep like a rock," said Margaret again, smiling proudly. "I sleep like a rock." And she answered every question after that with the same line, until she was instructed to leave with Ella.

Deliberation and decision were quick. Unless more evidence came to light, the two boys were pronounced guilty only of breaking curfew, and of breaking cubicle sanctity. As minors, they would be subject to a reduced sentence, converted into overtime staff duty, probation, extended curfew, and strict supervision by their respective Elders.

Mem Dora Prite was guilty of breaking the same codes. As an adult her sentencing was stricter: public censure and indefinite probation. She would no longer be allowed to visit other residential compounds.

Both cases would be reviewed in three months.

Elder Johnson concluded the proceedings.

"Mem Dora," he said, "ours is a sacred charge, to preserve and protect life in this colony. We are, in all of human history, set most apart from our mother lands. Ours is a new wilderness, and our task to give example and succor to the young. Like the Pilgrim Fathers who landed not two hundred miles from here, we have a destiny to fulfill—"

"Oh, bag it, will you?" said Mem Dora.

The room recoiled in shock. She arose, every ounce of her a bristling spectacle, a chain reaction of light and anger and self-possession. "In case you haven't noticed the color of my skin, Elder Johnson, it's black. My ancestors weren't among the Pilgrim Fathers; they were the slaves of the Virginia settlers and all their offspring. They weren't exactly bosom buddies. And they were kidnapped from Africa and the Caribbean, just as I was kidnapped and brought here. So I don't hold any truck with the Pilgrim Fathers routine. Get it?"

They shuffled their papers, stepped down. The meeting adjourned itself with a whimper.

16/ Making Up

The next afternoon, as Ella was on her way home from her assignment, she was surprised to see Mart lingering near the entrance to the glass garden. "Waiting for you," he said.

"None the worse for wear, I see," said Ella.

"Let's stop being mad at each other, it's so tiring," he said.

Ella felt wary for a moment. Forthright Mart wasn't necessarily trustworthy Mart. But talk about tiring: The recent days of being more or less alone with everything that had happened had wrung her out. Sorb's lisopress treatment and its worrying hold on him. Mem Dora's revelation about her past and the fate of Ella's parents. And this most recent—and terrible—adventure, which seemed miraculously to have ended without harm to anyone. Ella missed that part of Mart who was a true friend. She was ready to forgive him.

"I'm sorry for being harsh," she said.

"Me too. And for being heartless."

"Oh, Mart," she said with relief, "I don't really know if you're heartless. I just don't understand your heart all the time, that's all."

They headed down a hall, taking a long route so they could talk. For a while they lingered in neutral conversation, as if they were adults keeping life-and-death issues hidden under the scrim of everyday banter. How was he? How was she? Wasn't Mon Draper crabby in class today? Who ever could be expected to remember boring stuff like that for a surprise quiz?

Without speaking about it, they paused in a seldom-used stairwell and then surveyed each other for a minute or two, like nine year olds deciding whether or not to be friends.

Mart smiled first, and said softly, "Ella, let's go back north. Come on, no thinking or worrying about it, let's just do it."

He was such a doll now, how could she refuse him? Standing there at the iron balustrade, leaning just slightly toward her, hands clasped in a casual, almost feminine way on the rail. His tunic collar was open and his bare hairless torso showed in a chevron pointing down, the color of cream, paper, rising moons. He was going all-out with the charm, to win her back, and with Sorb so changed lately, she felt susceptible.

For a minute or two.

"I don't think I can go back there again," she said.

"You think I'm a lunatic for wanting to try so soon after being almost caught—"

124

"I think you're a full-time lunatic, Mart."

"It's even more important to me now, though." He wrenched at her with his look of puzzlement, appealing to her for this. "I want to hear you play. You wouldn't really play the other times—and can't you see it means a lot to me to hear you? You think I don't know who you are—"

"No, I don't."

"Yes, you do, and sometimes, I think you're right. But snag it all! To hear you play would give me something of you that you couldn't tell me with words. Don't you know what I mean? Doesn't that make sense?"

It made dangerously accurate sense. Ella felt chilled that he could read her so well.

"You have a death wish, Mart," she said. "You want to get fried by the lisopress like Sorb? Like Garner Jones, maybe? You have the luck of a seventh son and you push it to the absolute limit. Now sit down on that step there. I want to stop talking about us and talk about something more important."

"Come sit next to me," he said.

"Stop that. This is important."

They sat still for a while, composing themselves, keeping a careful half a dozen inches or so apart. How far from someone did you need to be to keep apart from the aromatic heat of their skin? Ella shifted away, cautiously, trying not to let Mart see.

"So what's the chat about?" he said.

She tried to think a clear path through the tangled thicket of her concerns. "Mart, why did you escape the lisopress treatment?"

"The Council of Elders found us not guilty of breaking drylock. You know that."

She felt stumped already. Tried again. "What was Sorb's crime, so bad it had to be punished by the lisopress?"

"You're asking rhetorical questions. You know as well as I that the Council of Elders never disclosed that information. Sorb says it was because he wouldn't gossip with his workmates. But Elder Saint Gabriel never came up with a reason, far as I've ever heard. So why *did* Sorb get lisopressed, Ella? You've obviously got an opinion."

She didn't want to say. She wanted Mart to say it aloud. If her idea was a crazy, loopy mistake, it would sound so in Mart's voice. "Wait. Let me start over. What do the people who've been through the lisopress treatment have in common?"

"Well. Let me see." Mart reached out to play with her curls, but she shook her head and he got the message. After a minute he said, "So far as I can see, no pattern at all."

"Oh, you're going to make me say it. All right. Mart, I can think of seven people who've been liso-pressed since we dug ourselves in here. Five of them were our age."

"So what? Kids are naturally disobedient."

"How many kids our age are there in the colony? Not many—maybe twelve. Five out of twelve is nearly fifty percent, Mart. Doesn't that strike you as suspicious?"

"Suspiciously what?"

"Mart!"

"Well, say it, say what you want, Ella, I don't get the point."

She ringed her hands around her ankles and leaned forward, saying softly, "We've been in this colony for almost five years. Some form of atomic explosion occurred five years ago that collapsed the escape tunnels of this place, and reduced our chances of emerging back into the world again to a feeble zero. We're so lucky, though, aren't we? Equipped with a life-support system more advanced than any space ship or colony has ever had. Mart, why aren't people clamoring to get out of here? Why do we live in a twenty-first-century catacomb with all the oomph and initiative of a sack of flour?"

"The tunnels are solid rock, Ella. You know that as well as I—"

"I know as well as you *what they say.* Why haven't there been attempts to dig our way out of here? Why have we settled in so happily, cursed by all these rules, why haven't people challenged the authority of the Council of Elders? My parents did resistance work—so did Mem Dora and her husband, the senator. Where are the resisters here?"

"I don't know."

"You do know. You're being stupid."

"Tell me, then."

"It's Sorb, you idiot. Sorb was beginning to resist. He was always one to say what was on his mind, but lately what was on his mind was *why are we still here?* You remember hearing about that Episode, where he proposed a lottery to elect someone to ask that question in public? And he's never let anyone forget about Garner Jones."

"What are you getting at, Ella Mencken?"

"I think Sorb was beginning to be capable of spearheading a movement to leave the Colony—"

"*Sorb?* He's a puppy! You're—"

"Listen to me. It might have taken some time, but I think the people who watch such things were noticing. Let me ask some more questions—I'm thinking out loud now. Why are fifty percent of the teenagers lisopressed? Why isn't there any opposition to the idea of our living here forever, until we're dug out? And why weren't you lisopressed for breaking out of drylock, Mart, which is a more serious crime than anything Sorb did or Garner Jones?"

"They couldn't prove it."

"But they know you did it. You know and they know you did it. Now I want you to tell me where you went, and why, but first I want you to think about this."

"Wait. Wait. Answer some of your questions first, Ella, you're losing me."

Trying to sound normal, trying to keep her voice from shaking. "Isn't it strange that four hundred people have stopped dreaming for five years? They bow to curfew, they accept the authority of the Council about everything. They believe the statements about the tunnels being impassable. What if they're not? Why aren't we trying to dig ourselves out anyway?"

"Tell me, don't ask questions—"

"I don't have the answers!" Her voice was an ugly hiss, she didn't care. "But I think Sorb was onto something. The adults aren't lisopressed because—they don't pose any threat. None of them asks any questions. No one but Mem Dora has ever so much as curled a lip at the Council of Elders. And that's another thing—if she was such a famous resister in her day, why hasn't she ever spoken up against the Council of Elders until now? She's like a cardboard cutout of the protester she used to be—"

"If it's a losing proposition—who wants to waste their energy?" Mart shrugged, dismissing Mem Dora.

"Talk about wasted energy! Nobody *does* anything here except hang around and wait to die! Mart, I'm tired of beating around the bush. This is what I think. You might not agree, but you're a resister too. You had the gumption to break out of drylock, and you got caught. But they didn't lisopress you. Why not?

"I'll tell you why not," she went on. "Because of one thing: Mem Dora was part of your alibi."

"What has that got to do with anything?"

"I've started asking people to talk about her. She's the original Witch Woman, they say; she's a famous figure from the past. Mem Lotus told me that Mem Dora and her husband had between them galvanized a mass demonstration against the idea of the colonies—a half a million people in Central Park gathered to hear him talk, and her sing. The famous Morning Star. She hasn't opened her mouth once since we got in here, not to sing, not to protest—not a word.

Just enough conversation to get by. Until this moment! And I think the Council of Elders is scared of her, scared she'll start a movement to overthrow their command. So they backed down from lisopressing you as soon as you produced her as an alibi."

"She's never made any trouble before. You're in outer space, Ella. Did she protest when Sorb was lisopressed, or Garner Jones, or anyone else? Has she ever made a single complaint about how things are run here?"

"But that's the thing: *She's made trouble now.* She *did* come to your defense. I bet the Council of Elders is quaking in their boots that she'll start stirring things up."

"Ella, you're romanticizing her beyond belief. She's a selfish dried-out rind of a woman. Her alibi was great, don't get me wrong, but she doesn't think about anything beyond Margaret, and sometimes not even that far."

"She's refused to sing for five years, even though she's a professional singer. Why?"

"There go your questions again. You tell me."

"I don't know, Mart. I'm not making up stories, I'm just thinking what I can think about all this. I think we should find out, if we can. It's not just idle curiosity—I have a feeling you need to protect yourself. You're next on some list, I'll bet it. One more misstep and you're fried."

"You've got a new kind of paranoia, that's what I think," said Mart, making it sound as if it were an attractive quality. "I don't buy all this, that the Council of Elders is trying to suppress anyone—"

130

"I don't think they mean any harm, but they're still the ones who keep anyone from trying to get out of here. *Has* anyone ever tried? Maybe they have and we just don't know. Maybe they're keeping the information from us."

"Maybe they did and died a horrible death, and the Elders are suppressing that so we don't all go mad with fear."

"We have a right to know even that," said Ella. "We have a right to fear, we have a right to dream. Isn't it strange that four hundred people have stopped dreaming for five years? Except Sorb, weird Sorb. Lisopressed Sorb. Maybe kids are lisopressed because they're still brave enough to fear, or antsy enough to dream."

"I never dream."

"Me either. Nor does anyone else. And as we get older, Mart, unless we're lisopressed into submission, we're just going to get gooder and goodor. More and more docile, I mean. Like Mon Conway—when he was in class with us he was a real comic. Now he's a j-guard, nasty as the lot."

"He was nice enough to Sorb and me when we were awaiting trial."

"He's a rat. He's been snowed under by all this, same as we will be if we don't watch out."

Mart was silent for a while. "Your saying all this is a preface to something, and I don't like it. You're about to say you don't want to risk breaking drylock again."

"Well, I don't think we should. They'll just be waiting to get you on something—"

"They haven't caught me yet."

"Yes, they did. You got stuck outside drylock all night. That's being caught, in my book. They just didn't charge you with it. Now let's not argue about this. Tell me where you and Sorb went that night. Did you go up to the piano?"

He smiled. "You're jealous."

"I am not."

"I told you what happened, we got caught outside drylock. We were late getting back and the evening drylock equation had snapped into place, and I've never been able to figure that one out."

"But why were you late?" she said. "Where did you stay? Why had you brought Sorb, when he's been so strange lately?"

"You were the one who accused me of heartlessness," he said. "So I was proving to myself and to Sorb and to you that I wasn't. I was giving him the gift of breakout. Only it backfired."

"I don't believe it."

"Why not?"

This was the part of Mart she hated. He was asking *Why not?* to see where his story was weak, so he could bolster it up. Not to see why she didn't believe it, and then be truthful about it. "Don't lie to me, Mart. That's not your kind of gesture, that's why not. Breaking drylock was a big private thing for you and you saved it for me. I know you and Sorb were— are—good friends, but you always treated him as if he were a disease. I don't believe your big turn-around."

132

"I wanted to impress you," he said. "It was important to me. I was depressed that you thought I was a scum. So I was out to make myself look good in your eyes. But it backfired. Don't you know how much I want you to like me?"

"That's a different question. We were talking about what happened that night."

"You're afraid Sorb and I got romantic ourselves and left you out of it."

"You're really stretching things," she said, although that thought had occurred to her, and not much bothered her, either. "You could get romantic with him or anyone else in an amity room. You don't need to put your whole life in jeopardy for that. Besides, that'd be a pretty extreme way of proving to me that you and Sorb were friends again and thus winning my approval and unfailing love, wouldn't it?"

He laughed at that. "Well, come closer and I'll tell you."

Payment due. She moved near him and listened to his whisper.

17/ At the Hatch

Once through drylock, Mart told her, on that early evening four days ago, he and Sorb had gone along the southeast equator route—a major track in the Reaches that led to chemical and electrical supply bins, relatively well traveled by the carters and their accompanying j-guards. It was, in fact, the metal access passage to the entrance hatch in the permaderm, the hatch through which the colonists had entered their living grave.

Mart didn't know the path well. In his own scramblings he'd avoided it because of the traffic, preferring the quieter northern and southern Reaches. But Sorb, Mart said, had been gripped by a quiet curiosity during the week following his lisopress treatment. He'd consistently asked for the "stragglers"—but he wouldn't define what he meant except to say "those who fell along the way—they come in dreams." It'd taken Mart several days to guess that Sorb meant the way into the Centrex globe—so in an effort to break his obsession, he was taking Sorb out to see that route, from the entrance hatch through the equatorial Reaches right up to drylock, to prove that no one had fallen along the way.

(Ella didn't remember very much of what that route looked like. She, along with so many others, measured time from day one, week one, when they'd milled into the gallery and been given temporary assignments in random compounds until the corrected arrangements could be made. Mart told Ella that it was a route far more brightly lit and better kept than the out-of-the-way northern Reaches Ella knew. The metal road was clear of dust, the bins and cages electronically guarded and flooded with light.)

Sorb had peered between the cages, in the metal gutters and sudden drops along the road, scrutinizing the right-hand Reaches. Mart hadn't been the soul of patience, he admitted to Ella, asking and then demanding to know what Sorb was looking for. Sorb had merely answered, "Stragglers, that's all, just in case," and had been unperturbed at Mart's impatience—no unusual thing, for Sorb.

By the time they'd reached the entrance hatch in the permaderm, Mart knew that it was likely they'd be late, and miss the change in drylock equation, and be locked out.

He tried to hurry Sorb, who was fascinated by the entrance hatch.

It looked like an oversize medieval shield, oddly wider at the top than at the bottom, encrusted with a cloisonné-bright complexity of electronic and physical locks, systems, restraints, and calendars. Dull-blue metallic skin studded with pirate's jewels of ruby, amethyst, amber, and turquoise: the flickering lights of the post-and-lintel computer warning-and-guarding arrangement.

Sorb went right up to it, and ran his hands along its richly textured surface. Mart was horrified—but no alarms were sounded, at least in their hearing. No joltings happened, nothing dreadful.

Sorb wanted to know what was on the other side.

You know what, said Mart. Four hundred thousand tons of dirt. You remember.

But Sorb said he was concerned for those who'd fallen by the wayside in the tunnel. He wanted to get out to see them. They might need some help.

Mart went furious then, cursing Sorb up and down for his stubborn blindness and this giddy new silliness. He threatened to turn around and leave Sorb there—to die, in fact, because Sorb would never be able to get through drylock alone—or to be picked up by j-guards. But Sorb didn't even bother to answer his threats.

What if there's someone on the other side of this hatch, trying to get in?

Knock it down, Sorb suddenly cried. Tear it apart!

He crumpled himself up against the door, on his knees, saying he could tell there were stragglers on the other side waiting to get in. We've got to open it up, he said, we've got to get them to open it up. We'll go to the Council of Elders and talk them into it. There

136

have been people waiting for five years to get in here, it's not right to be so selfish.

(Ella said, "Are you fabricating this right before my very eyes, Mart? When I've just gone on and on about people not having the nerve to resist?" Mart swore that he wasn't. Ella didn't know if she believed him or not. Sorb having a perfect fit wasn't so incredible, these days, but Mart being patient enough to wait through it, to stand it, was almost beyond belief.)

He'd comforted Sorb. Years ago, he'd said, there was no space travel. We were trapped on the earth like monkeys on a tropical island, and we waited for centuries for the idea of flight to develop. We are trapped here in no more frightening a way than our ancestors were.

(Ella asked Mart if he believed that. We're the living dead, he told her, but I had to say something.)

Sorb eventually grew calmer. He stretched out along the bottom edge of the door, as if in his sleep he might wisp smokily under the crack and through the tunnel and out, and Sorb fell asleep, with Mart sitting near him.

Mart was afraid to sleep. It was pretty certain that j-guards didn't patrol out of drylock, and in the night there'd be no carters at work in the Reaches. By now the hour had passed in which a safe journey home would have been possible; they were out for the night. Mart was only afraid that his compound residents would report his absence, and very soon Sorb's would be reported, too. J-guards out at night, hunting for them in the Reaches. . . .

As he sat watching over Sorb, the two of them like beggars at an ancient gate to a Middle Eastern city, he mulled over lots of things. With sleepiness letting down his guard, he regarded the intricacies of the hatch, its locks and systems. Without even knowing what he was doing, he studied the comings and goings of prods and circuits, mistral paths and lorimar angles.

"I figured it out," he said to Ella.

"You figured what out?"

"How the hatch works."

She couldn't see his face, suddenly, so sure was she that he was lying.

He must've picked up her doubt and scorn. "Well, not how to open it. Not like drylock. But I could see how it must work. It's really pretty easy. It's two drylock systems, one inverted over the other, and an accompanying net ripple guard—probably set on a grid pattern of infinite combinations. But I could see that if you had the right information and a few universal tools—"

She hardly knew what to think, so worried about the weirdness of Sorb. So unlike Mart, all this! And yet, who was she to say what he was like or not? Had his kindness to Sorb been part of his own unspoken anxiety about the mess Sorb was in? How odd that it had come at the same time as her own fledgling attempts at understanding, rejecting what was lousy, and investigating what was left. . . .

"Now, will you go north," Mart whispered, "since I've given you all this juicy news?"

138

"Only on my own," she answered. "If you want to get me through drylock, I'll go north and play by myself. But I won't let you take me there. I won't take the responsibility of having you usher me there, Mart, because you'll get juiced in an instant if you're found."

His face went dark with anger when he saw, after all this revelation, she was going to hold her own. "G—," he began to swear at her, checked himself, and invented a new curse. "Garner you!" he said.

PART THREE

Back in the ice maze again. Twisted corridors of white, opaque as the cooked white of an egg, blind as the ovoid white of an eye, hard as the lasting white of a bone. Who shrieks and moans for Garner Jones?

He was running, sliding, ricocheting through the maze now. Not so much scared of hairy demons or hopeful of angel assistance, but simply running, searching, for the ones he'd left behind. Devil and angel alike begone: It was the human cost that moved him now.

They'd left the transport unit and joined the throngs pulsing westward toward the Pioneer Colony. Its exact location had been kept a secret, but rumor had moved the thousands to search, and so the road that Sorb and his parents were taking— the true road, the right road, because Sorb's father knew—*was choked with desperate pilgrims. Hur-*

tling like forest animals before a fire. Clawing like crabs, pinching, pillaging—not for food, or clothing, or rape, but for simple shelter from the hardest storm the earth would ever see. Houses, warehouses, outhouses, any houses in the Pioneer Valley seemed safer than anywhere else, by dint of their nearness to the secret colony. Maybe safety would spread its wings over them, too.

But Sorb had kept on, and on, having been told of the exact location, having memorized the directions. And when the October snow had piled cold gray powder ankle deep, and he'd stopped to breathe an instant before running on, he'd turned and realized they weren't there behind him. Daddy, Mommy—trampled underfoot? Lost?

But he'd kept on, choosing life, or so he'd said to himself later, before the amnesia of a new society had taken over and helped him forget. He'd found the secret entrance, presented the phony datacard, slipped in over the threshold. Just twenty or thirty minutes before the hatch had been closed, as the full-scale attack was about to begin.

One of four hundred who made it, when the Colony had facilities for a thousand.

Through such a race, and at such a cost, he'd managed to lock himself in a maze of ice. But he couldn't stay any longer.

Because now he could see them again, after all these years. Huddled up on the other side of the hatch, still tapping at the gate. Her arm was around his waist; she'd dragged him all the way though he was twice her size. She said, You did what you must and we don't accuse—but Sorb, Sorba, darling child: It's time to leave. You must come out. It's time to live. You must come out.

So he was running, slipping, catapulting against the frigid menace of the maze. And he would mate with the devil or murder the angel, if that's what he had to do to get out. Because it was no longer possible to forget the parents he'd so necessarily forgotten.

If nothing else, he would get out just to burn their bones, in a final act of blazing against all that had choked and frozen them to death.

18/ The Haunting

Sometime in the weeks that followed—and later he could never pinpoint the time exactly—Sorb began to realize that Pioneer was haunted.

It started with a battery of dreams that came back to him during his waking hours, in one-dimensional jolts, like single chords extracted from a symphony, or tiny portions of color lifted from a large and dizzying canvas. He would hear a voice, or nearly hear it. His name would be said. *Sorb*. He'd sit upright at his console, thinking first that someone was speaking to him, but there'd be no one near. Then, he'd wonder if he'd dreamed of someone speaking his name. But the lisopress treatment had run long fingernails through his diaphanous dreams, and only shreds and tatters, senseless as they were, remained.

He tried to think objectively about whose voice might be calling him. *Sorb*. As he went through the motions of life in the Pioneer Colony, he listened to the voices around him that might be present also in his dreams. But it wasn't lovely Ella, nor Mart with the eyes like barbs of light. Nor little Margaret Prite, nor her controversial mother, Mem Dora. Nor loony Mem Lotus, nor fearsome Mem Wonski from work, nor Mon Draper, the teacher.

There wasn't much in his reserve of dreams with which to team up the voice. Where earlier he'd dreamed richly, of situations frightening, inexplicable, sexy, glorious, with a full palette of emotions and images, now he had only random pebbles by which to recall his dreams. A color, a shade, downtrodden by fake daylight, unrecognizable.

One evening at Episode, Mem Lotus decided to tell about an early point in her life, when she'd first met Mon Lotus and married him. Mon Lotus, a businessman, had met Mem Lotus in a New York urb coffee shop where, of all romantic situations, his wife-to-be was receiving a severe scolding by her boss. Mem Lotus, a waitress, had failed to clean out the coffee urn and, overnight, roaches had found their way into it. A roach came through the spigot into someone's ceramic mug.

"Oh, he was lousy to me. 'A college girl,' he said, 'don't know how to clean out a coffee urn! You should take your fancy credentials and find work somewhere else!' And work, let me tell you young things, wasn't easy to find when I was young. Well, I was in a tizzy. I swung around and beseeched—"

"You *beseeched*?" scoffed Mon Troy. "Shakespearian actress in a coffee shop, is that it?"

Mem Lotus, unmiffed, said, "I yelled, 'Is anyone

147

going to punch this bastard in the face for me? I'm too short to do it myself.' "

"And your future husband leaped up and punched him in the face," said Ella.

"No," said Mem Lotus, "he almost had a heart attack trying to get out the door before I asked again. He was the only man there but never felt fighting resolved anything. A large woman in gold jewelry stood up and said, 'Lay off, lout, or I ain't coming here for coffee and none of my friends ain't either.' So my boss fired me, and I huffed and puffed out of there, caught up with the chicken-hearted Boscar Lotus at the subway, and tripped him up. He fell down the stairs and broke his foot. I visited him in the hospital every day for a week and we got married a month later."

Sorb watched Ella watching Mem Lotus. Ella had a guarded look of satisfaction, as if she were smiling inside herself at the story. She had little Andrew Afshar in her arms, and she plumped him up and down and worked him into an ecstasy of coos and bubbles. Was it the voice Andrew would have, grown up, that Sorb heard every now and then when his body relaxed and his mind went waltzing out of the feature of the moment and into its own ellipses? Sorb tried to imagine Andrew grown. . . .

"Tell us about your wedding," said Ella.

"Well, travel was easier for everyone in those days. My uncle gave me away, dressed in his military space silvers, and my aunt snuffed loudly into her handkerchief and confided to everyone within fifteen pews

148

that it was about time I brought some money into the family. She was a fright, my aunt, a hat like a Spanish galleon sitting so high off her head that when she stood to witness it knocked against the chandelier and caught on fire. My uncle disgraced himself forever by letting out one small anemic guffaw for which my aunt never forgave him."

"But was it romantic?"

"Any wedding is romantic, dearie."

"Tell me about it," said Mon Troy dryly. "We were married in a truck stop, snowbound for two weeks up near Hudson Bay. There was a minister also snowbound, luckily. It was either that or start sinning to beat the band. Nothing else to do till the authorities dug us out."

Sorb said, "We're frozen stones, like Garner Jones." He didn't like the idea of being snowbound, for some reason.

"Was there champagne? Dancing?" said Ella.

"Oh, child!" Mem Lotus's face shone pink and brilliant. "When we left the chapel to go to our hired cars, there were children playing on the street. Playing Ghost, and the child who was It was hiding and counting. Boscar got a wild gleam in his eye, and we joined into the game, for three rounds, even with our wedding finery on."

"I never played Ghost," said Mem Waterhouse. "Papa didn't allow us to play street games."

"One child is chosen to be It," said Mem Lotus, "and hides Its eyes while counting to one hundred. Then It turns and says loudly, 'Star light, star bright,

I hope I see a Ghost tonight.' Then It tiptoes around as soft as It can through the neighborhood, looking for the hidden ones. If It sees one before It is seen, It calls out 'One two three four, Ghost Jim at my door,' or Ghost Debbie or Maureen or whoever. If It finds all the hiders, then It has won. It's not much of a game, as street games go, but did we love it that night!"

Sorb said to himself, One two three four, Ghost Someone at my door.

"Oh, yes," said Mem Lotus, "it was a wild time, for I was all in the traditional whites—veils and trails and silly ruffled skirts—hiding in the November dusk, all glowing as a ghost would, light from stores and streetlamps pooling in my clothes, hovering like a cloud of gnats around me. Boscar held my hand, the child roared out his line—"

"Star light, star bright," remembered Margaret promptly, "I hope I see a Ghost tonight—"

Sorb's eyes closed of their own accord, and inner screams rang out. He hadn't intended to close his eyes, but things were different now.

The ground in which Pioneer Colony was buried was crowded with ghosts.

He'd never thought of that before. As he'd been instructed, years ago, he'd learned to think of the enormous globe colony as being divorced from a context, as spaceships are, a mote in eternity, neighborless. The Pioneer colonists were as far from their pasts as Mars colonists. But in the involuntary closing of his eyes and the screaming of voices inside him, his sight suddenly expanded. It was as if the dial of a macroscope had been brutally wheeled from smallest to highest magnification, and he was nauseated with the change in field, reeling and blind to the new images on parade.

The paths of ghosts are like orbits of planets, protrinos, the circle of ocean currents: nearly impossible to divert. As fish move through water, ghosts transport through time and matter alike.

A school of ghosts encircled the Pioneer, traversing gravel, sand, limestone, the relaxed skeletons of humans and animals killed in the A-Day attack or earlier, traversing the wells and cellars and conduits of the dead world above.

The ghosts swarmed in shifting numbers. Sometimes there were a thousand, sometimes a thousand and one. Their ghostly congregation allowed for only a thousand former spirits, and an extra one had crowded its way into the streaming procession, constantly dislodging, ghost by ghost, essence from movement, like a never-ending game of musical chairs. It was the one rude intruder ghost who was speaking his name. *Sorb.* But the ghost was outside still, as they all were, enwreathing the enormous spherical tomb. How could he hear its voice alone from the rest? And why was its voice speaking his name?

Did ghosts have wings?

Above the dance of ghosts, on a flat wave of dirt and crumbling concrete and densasteel, the stage design consisted of dead buildings, withered trees, elegant loops of highway, and the fading light of the alphabet inscribed glowingly on everything. Strangely, he could see well. The detail of deteriorating lintels, the husks of mass-transit trains, the delicate pattern of the last traffic jam of all time burned into the skin of the roadways. But he couldn't tell if it was day or night. If there was light abroad or not. The horizon was the color of copper corrosion, that rich, felted green. No stars, no shadows. No sun, no glare.

Easy on the eyes.

Suddenly, as if from a helicopter, his vision began to swoop in, focus and move more specifically about the landscape. The details grew yet more precise—achingly so. A spray of human blood upon the side of a wall. A spare carcass in some protected cavern—an elevator?—twisted in on another two or three carcasses, like socks rolled together. A huge 3-D film marquee, old-fashioned style, dropped onto a public concourse like a massive block of ice, and the epitaph of the scene registered in sizzling letters: LOVE'S LABOUR'S LOST.

Sorb, said the ghost voice.

His eyes opened before he found what he was looking for, although he had no idea what that was.

The Jefferson residents were frozen with open mouths.

Had he screamed?

But they weren't looking at him. They looked at each other.

"Holy Jesus God Almighty," said Mem Lotus, "what the devil gives?"

There was a faltering chorus of screams and groans, a few senseless words, spittle and gasp. It matched the screams Sorb had heard when his eyes had suddenly closed of their own accord. "Ghosts," he said, matter-of-factly. Only Ella heard him, glared with fear at him, burst into tears, and fell on the floor, clutching Andrew Afshar in panic.

"I'm going up to Control," said Elder Saint Gabriel. "I'll go too," said Mon Troy. Mem Troy screamed for her husband not to leave. Mem Waterhouse was on her knees, eyes closed, lips trembling: "Out of the depths I have cried unto thee, O Lord."

Margaret alone seemed unimpressed. "What's going on?" she asked her mother.

Mem Dora gathered Margaret in her lap and sat very still. "We'll know sooner or later."

"It's ghosts," said Sorb, "that's all."

"It's not ghosts!" said Ella. "Shut up with the ghosts, Sorb!"

He didn't understand. "Well, what is it?"

Ella rose to her knees, rolling Andrew unceremoniously to the floor. "It's a break in the power, Sorb! The lights went off for a minute—all of them! Guard lights and night lights and everything!"

"Oh well, they'll fix that," said Sorb, a bit disappointed that it wasn't ghosts. Of course, he supposed it was serious that the lights had blinked. The Pioneer was supposed to be eternal, not even so much as a second's power lapse was supposed to be possible.

Still, ghosts were far more interesting. It wasn't electric power that kept speaking his voice, even though no one else seemed to hear it.

Mem Lotus said, "I want to go to the gallery, and hear what's happening. Maybe it was just our compound."

"Get Control on the diatone," insisted Mem Nazira, who had rescued Andrew from the floor. "There's no sense sitting here and twiddling our thumbs."

"But we can't get out!" said Mem Troy, more emotion in her voice than they'd ever heard.

She sat on the end of her bench next to Mon Gorky, her hands clasped as tightly as physiology would allow, her ordinary calm and slightly distracted demeanor shaken and flushed. Tears ran from her left eye. Her right eye was sealed in a crusty way. Her voice moved from ebb to flow with tears clogging the valves.

"We were never supposed to—to get trapped in here—it isn't fair—they ought to—held accountable—as if our lives were—beads for bartering—and if we ever could—the air might still be poison—all our treasures blasted to slivers—a joke, a colossal joke—"

Mem Lotus and Mem Dora went to her and held her, Mem Lotus saying, "No, dear, it's not at all like that, hope springs eternal," and Mem Dora gritting her teeth and saying nothing.

Sorb wasn't impressed. He turned to look at Ella, who still knelt on the floor, though not in prayer. She had her hands in her skirted lap, stiffly, and her lips were pressed together till they were almost colorless.

Maybe it was the extra ghost who was responsible for the break in power and light. He wondered how he could find out.

154

19/ The Acemyte
Harvesters

The following days were ragged. The Elders met, the engineers conferred and reported, the rumors flew and fell apart.

There had been a power (leak/surge). Some (foreign agent/colonist) had (fed into/stolen from) the (main generator/auxiliary generator) a (modest increment/fatal excess) of (primary chemical/secondary electrical) power which (could be overlooked by/was the kiss of death for) (all/some/none) of the Pioneer colonists.

No one was speaking officially to the public. The news sheets were flimsy on facts. "It is believed that engineers suspect either mechanical failure, outside interference, or inside sabotage." But the engineers were never quoted exactly about what they found, and the Elders adopted a similar noncommittal stance.

Mart, trudging from compound to compound on his food report collection assignment, found himself looking with greater care than usual at the behavior of the colonists. He saw evidence of fear: the chairs drawn closer together in most compounds, the rare and exotic beeswax candles brought out from storage and set in the centers of tables, the worn look on people's faces. There was a rising number of jokes about where to be when the lights went out the next time—and dwindling laughter at such jokes.

But. But. Could it be that Ella was really onto something? She'd been so positive that living in the Colony was fostering a kind of lethargy, a lack of action. If ever Mart would have expected people to rally together and demand information from the Council of Elders, it was now. Yet joking, gossip, idle speculation seemed to satisfy. No one seemed prepared to question the Council about what had really happened.

In such a curious vacuum of reaction, Mart's own feelings about the blackout were set in relief. He'd been petrified, naturally, when the lights had failed. Agnes Treasure, that royal pain, had been singing every nursery rhyme she knew, making herself the central character. "Little Agnes Moffat, Sat on a tuffet." "Mistress Agnes, Quite contrary." (How true.) "Agnes be nimble, Agnes be quick." And the lights, sardonic things, went out just as she'd concluded "Agnes jump over the candlestick." There'd been the silence of disbelief, and Mart had inserted his own little jab—"Well, Agnes, now's your chance"—and then the lights had roared on again, mercifully.

Being able to be mean to a little girl, however obnoxious, at a time of terror like that, was proof to Mart that he was himself gripped with horror.

Challenged by Ella to pay attention to such things, he made a decision, part in fun and part in anxiety, to look at what he saw in the colony. If he and Ella were the only likely revolutionaries, he wanted to play the part well. It would at least keep her talking to him, since she seemed to be drifting away so slowly but certainly. . . .

One afternoon his assignment was to go to the nursery hall and collect information on the rate of acemyte harvesting. It would be a long and tedious job, but the glass garden was situated off to one side, and maybe he'd catch sight of Ella.

Six workers managed the daily acemyte harvest. Acemyte was the most important source of nourishment to the colonists, and the workers were often supervised by the j-guards. The acemyte grew in crimped green furls, like small flags rolled up together around a slender central stick, twelve heads to a glass tray, regular as buttons on a vest. The trays smelled terrible, flushed constantly with a solution of water and chemical nutrients. The older colonists said that the glass field smelled like an antique darkroom. But nothing dark about it—a tireless light beat down endlessly from the racks of torpa lamps hung from the steel-beamed ceiling.

The work was hard and couldn't be done by machine. Had the designers of the Pioneer Colony not feared the insect above all else, the tiny Brazilian contraslugs could have been imported, to do their slow eating-dance around the base of the acemyte. This caused the furls to fall outward, like the petals of a rose, exposing them to more light, faster growth: a more abundant harvest. But Brazilian contraslugs and all other insects were banned categorically from the days of the Colony's construction. Human beings could put up with scandalous conditions for unimaginable lengths of time. The possibility of being overrun by bugs in an underground colony was not one of them.

As Mart went from tray to tray, noting the state of the individual acemyte plants with a metal notcher on a flexible wheel, he watched the six harvesters slowly twirling individual plants in their glass wells, separating the roots to insure proper feeding, pulling with agonized gentleness the ripe leaves from the outside of the fragrant green cylinders.

Mon Conway was stalking around the far end of the hall. Mart took care to keep his back turned as often as possible. No sense in a confrontation.

One woman—her name, Mart thought, was Mem Bettina—had an old-timer's kerchief tied around her head, from which a feathery fringe of shockingly pale hair tufted, forehead and nape. "You must be one of the regulars," he said to her.

"Ja, ja," she said, "my hair it blinds you, no? It turns white by the torpa light."

"How can you do this every day and not go crazy?"

"I am singing to myself all the time. The funny old songs of the old place, way north in farming land. I never remember the name of the district, just it is home." Mem Bettina picked with swollen fingers that stank of chemicals. "Like my mother's favorite song.

158

'God Mercy on the Slow of Heart.' You know this song?"

"No." Mart thought: a new song I could tell Ella about. "Sing it."

She lifted her head, took her hands from the plant, and dropped a leaf in her humidified cart. She turned her head to look for Mon Conway, and in a small voice she sang:

> *"God mercy on the slow of heart,*
> *The hard of hand who slap and sting,*
> *They do not know the pain they start,*
> *Nor understand the death they bring.*
> *And if the mercy of the Lord*
> *Will not apply to villains—well,*
> *Then may they get their just reward—"*

She gave a little grin.

> *"And rot their stinking souls in hell."*

Mart tried to keep from laughing. No believer he, but the joke was good. Mem Bettina moved on to the next plant. "So why should I not enjoy my work, yes? I am amusing myself at every time."

"I've got to move on."

"Perhaps if you are here later, we meet for tea and larmer with the others. We have rest soon. Yes?"

He nodded, and drifted away. The acemyte harvesters were all like her, older people, for whom moving down the aisles of glass trays was a difficult and exhausting job. When the bell rang for tea and

159

larmer, Mart watched them come to the center area with slow steps, tired arms, glances that met each other only after a cup had been carefully prepared, and a spot found on the metal bench, and shoes eased off with a sigh. Why didn't they refuse to do this drudgery?

Mon Conway was there, and he and Mart avoided looking at each other although they stood hip to hip and shoulder to shoulder, preparing their cups from the same row of ingredients. Mart felt a new and severe suspicion of Mon Conway, no matter how nice he'd been gossiping with him and Sorb the other evening. Mon Conway had a bloated sort of righteousness of the kind Ella was trying to point out. He was part of the structure of normalcy. It would be good to stay out of his way.

The conversation was slow in starting. Mem Bettina winked at Mart and said to Mon Conway, "You dig up any criminals today, young man?" Mon Conway just grunted. A bald man said, "Don't bother the j-guard, Mem Bettina, he's resting."

"So excuse me! Of course. Even the law must rest from time to time."

"I have bumps on my ankles," said an old woman.

"Bumps on my knees, from bumping into that stupid cart."

"They should give us chairs to sit on. Chairs with wheels."

"Absolutely so."

"They probably got some up in the Reaches, Mon j-guard, sir?"

Mon Conway sipped, sighed, and said, "Lots of stuff."

"Sounds to me like you don't know," said an old woman. "Just gassing around about it. Hmmm?"

"It's confidential," murmured Mon Conway.

"They should bring us chairs. If they got 'em," said the old woman. She looked at Mart. "You think they got chairs up there?"

"Oh, I don't know," said Mart. "Maybe they've got stuff besides chemicals and equipment. Maybe they have wild things—like rocking horses. Or pianos. Or books."

"Ah, books! You should say the magic word. Sure they remembered to bring sixty tons of computers, but they forgot the books. They got books up in the Reaches, it's a crime. I've read my old collected tales of Edgar A. Poe so often you can see through the paper."

"No books, I'm sure," said Mon Conway decisively. "Just supplies. Nothing worth breaking out of drylock and stealing, you know."

Mart turned an innocent face on Mon Conway. He let his eyes open a bit wider than usual, his jaw drop a half an inch or so. "Of course I was acquitted on that charge," he said lightly. But Mon Conway had directed attention to him; the acemyte harvesters were looking at him differently now. "Ja, ja, I recognize him, so what, nothing proven," protested Mem Bettina mildly. "A hundred people a day accused of crimes they never did, it's the natural way, so what's to be fussy about?" She tugged at her scarf, pulling it a little lower on her head, as if to keep out the sound of her colleagues' grousing.

"They never asked me," said Mon Conway in a conversational tone, leaning over toward Mart, "but I could have told them that back when I was in Mon Draper's classroom, I could see you doing Kopol equations at the age of twelve. All Mon Draper could do was look dimly at your page and say, 'Now do you understand how that works?' because it was so far beyond him. You figured it out pretty quickly, didn't you, to keep that talent hidden?"

"Only devious minds think like that," said Mart, pretending quiet righteousness even though, in fact, Mon Conway had the truth to a tee. "The advanced manual on Kopol equations and stuff like persistence of ebronic equality came to an end eventually and there was nothing else to do. So I gave up on it."

"Could you break into the air tally system?"

"What an odd request," said Mart, stunned. Why was he asking this? "You have something in mind?"

"No. No, I just can't figure those things out. And if you're half as good now as you used to be, it should come as a snap to you."

Mart remembered Ella's warnings. "You're doing double duty as a detective," he said, as if joking, "trying to prove I have the capability of real serious crime."

"Oh, come on," snorted Mon Conway. "I'm just wondering, is all."

"Well, what possible good would it do either of us to break into the air tally system? Either we'd set off the alert by accident, and get in lots of trouble, or we

162

would gape like a couple of chimpanzees at the inner mechanics of it and close it up and be no smarter. I happen to think that the air tally register is a good machine *not* to tamper with. These people need"— and he made his voice louder—"they need to rely on the air tally system so that they know they're not being poisoned. It's not a good suggestion."

"Hold on," said Mon Conway. "I didn't suggest you do it. I just asked you if you could."

"Who should want to mess with the air tally register?" said an old man. "We'd be dropping like flies if the chemical flush in the water accidentally increased. You are hanging around longer than you're supposed to, you're making bad news." He wagged a finger. "I think you should go on and bother someone else. Aren't you on a schedule?"

"Ah, leave him be to rest his feet," said someone.

"No, go on, we don't need bullying and fooling with our air tally. We rely on it," said the old man. "Maybe you go on too, Mart Rengage. You got the stamp of the old Morning Star on you now and to my nose it stinks."

Mon Conway arose. Mart said, "I've got work to do here yet." If this had been a little game, neither he nor the j-guard had won. Mon Conway wandered off, looking perhaps a little lonely for just a minute. Mart sat and wondered if Ella's paranoia was contagious, and if he'd needlessly accused the j-guard of prying.

In the distance, he heard Mon Conway arriving at the door to the glass garden, and the shrill denial of his request for entrance. Mem Gesevich was in high good spirits; she could be heard down to the last syllable.

Ella'd be in there, he knew, wincing in memory of the time that she'd broken down and let Mon Conway in. The first intrusion of a j-guard in the glass garden. She talked about it still, with alternating defensiveness and shame. She took those children to her heart, counted them among her friends. Mart was even jealous of them. He knew that jealousy got in the way; he would love her best when he didn't hate her for her large talent for kindness—for the kids, for Sorb, and lately, for Mem Dora.

When he went to rinse out his cup, he found that the conversation had turned to the quiet woman. As usual, once she became the center of conversation, he was let off the hook; the colonists seemed to blame her for the seduction of the two boys, and he and Sorb had almost entirely escaped public censure.

"She's a witch. She's the original Witch Woman," said the old man who'd asked Mart to leave. "How she's even kept as low a profile as she has here, I'll never know. It's just witchery. A woman like that."

"She sings like an angel," said Mem Bettina. "Even I know that. I never see a chemistrix of her, nor I ever go to a show. Or a rally. But I hear her singing some nonsense on the public access station once and I think: My dear, this is what the angels are going to sound like when you get there. That is, if I don't rot my stinking soul in hell." She winked at Mart.

"She's a lady Hitler, she's another Bertha Gamble,

she has the souls of a billion people on her conscience, and she sleeps with minors!" spat the old man.

Mart didn't move. He seldom heard invectives like these.

"Oh, it's how you cut the pie—"

"The pie is already cut, and we get the last crumb known to history, and the rest of it is rotted away, no thanks to her. Sure, she can sing. So Hitler could dance, too, you remember from those antique pictures? And Bertha Gamble could ride a bicycle, so what?"

"You fuss, what's the fuss?" said Mem Bettina. "Just we're the new animals in the new ark, is all. We can't blame one lady for people's lives, you're acting cranky. Have you taken your mistricle tablet today? Go on, take."

The rest time was over. The old people were rising, rinsing cups, cracking knuckles and rubbing inflamed skin, and moving back to their places in the glass field. Mart looked at the time, and realized he couldn't afford to stop and say hello to Ella. Or to tell her what had happened, and that he was starting to be convinced that she was right. They were all bowing slowly under the weight of their death sentence, hardly realizing it. No one had mentioned the energy lapse. Already it was past history, and things were back to normal: kneeling on the ground, yoke on the shoulders. Even these old people, tart as ginger, back to work in the fields as if they were slaves, and no end in sight.

As he left, he heard one woman complaining to a

friend, "If you ask me, she shouldn't have been allowed in here in the first place. There were billions of other people who had a better right to her place here. They should have left her and her daughter out. Take *that*, and see how it feels."

God mercy on the slow of heart, he thought, all irony from that line draining away.

20/ Mem Ella Mencken

Suddenly, with an uncharacteristic disregard for her responsibilities, Mem Gesevich keeled over and died. Just like that, while having her breakfast in Colwell Compound.

Mem Lotus, who took the call on the diatone, turned and said to Ella, "They want you, dearie, the Elders do. In the Council Room at noon." She raised an eyebrow to show how impressed she was at the turn of events. "Ella and the Elders. Knock 'em dead, sweetie."

"Oh, Ella, I'm so sorry," said Mem Dora. But Ella had to turn her face away, because she had no real sorrow to show, just a blank look of exhaustion, and she was ashamed.

But as she dressed carefully for her appointment with the Elders, having pressed her serviceable canvas skirt till the edges seemed alert enough to withstand another A-Day attack, she could only think coldly of Mem Gesevich. She saw her waking up, yawning, boring everyone at Colwell Compound with her recital of the day's goals. She saw her pitching forward on the table, or backward against the wall, her face gone white as strongpoint enamel, her strange apricot hair looking pinker than ever by contrast. She saw her carried away on a deadsheet that would, according to Mon Troy, be washed and folded and put again on the shelf. She saw her being tilted awkwardly into the chiller, naked as a babe, freckled with the soft beige pox that seemed to plague older people lingering too long underground.

"You're very upset," said Mem Dora, hanging around at the door, arms folded severely across her bosom.

Ella didn't answer.

"She was a very good woman."

"She was a crank," said Ella, "but a good strong one. How do I look?"

"Loosen your collar. The shirt's too tight and it pinches you."

I'm growing, thought Ella, all my clothes are too small. Maybe the Elders are going to assign me some of Mem Gesevich's clothes to make over for myself.

"We can talk later, before our lesson."

"I don't particularly *want* to *talk*." This was great, having Mem Dora be chatty for the first time in five years at the one time when it wasn't welcome. Ella considered saying something quiet but friendly, to show that her rejection of Mem Dora wasn't personal, and then thought, *Oh, hell, skip it.* She left her cubicle and Mem Dora behind, and started off toward the Council Room with her heart useless and heavy inside her.

The Elders were arranged around the council table. Tight little polite smiles twisted onto their faces like bow ties. A sameness in the expression: Leadership is hard, no one knows but us, but we bear it all uncomplainingly, for *you.*

Their request was simple and directly put. Would Ella take over the leadership of the glass garden? Mem status would be conferred if she would.

Mon Draper, her teacher, was there and made a suggestion that Ella wasn't mature enough for the job. His objection was overruled.

"I'll do it," Ella said dully, and the traditional gavel thudded onto a square of cobalt-blue flannel.

"Recess," ordained Elder Johnson, and then Ella said, "Wait. One provision."

The Elders, in the act of rising, set themselves down again. They did not mask their curiosity.

"Ever since I received my assignment to assist Mem Gesevich in the glass garden," said Ella, "we've had to deal with the j-guards coming by, almost daily, trying to bluster their way in and maybe even do those awful mestrol checks on the kids. Mem Gesevich was a powerhouse in dealing with them, but she was sixty pounds heavier than I am and could have wrestled any one of them to the floor. I can't. I want a ruling that makes the glass garden off-limits for j-guards."

169

"You can't just ask for rulings like that," said Elder Moxie-doxie. "What does Mon Draper teach you in civics class, anyway? A ruling is proposed by a member of the Council of Elders. You're out of order to make such a proposal."

"I might not know civics, but I know kids and I know myself," she answered calmly, "and putting up with that threat daily is more than I could handle."

"Irregular. An arrogant request," murmured Elder Johnson, as if about to reconsider the appointment.

"I so propose," said old Elder Zink, straightening her papers, "that j-guards be instructed to consider the glass garden off-limits during hours of operation, except during an emergency."

The other Elders swallowed their objections, voted and accepted the resolution, and Elder Johnson said, with irritation, "We are now adjourned."

"I would also like to know why we need j-guards at all anymore—" said Ella.

"We are now *adjourned*," said Elder Johnson, and stamped his gavel twice.

Elder Saint Gabriel came forward and pressed Ella's hand warmly. "You'll be a credit to us all in Jefferson, Ella, I'm quite sure."

"It's so sudden," she said.

"In good time you'll be comfortable. Shall we walk back to the compound? My duties here are concluded for now."

She wanted to walk alone, to go hide in an amity room and examine her reactions to all this, but her reactions seemed anemic and unworthy of the effort. So she said she would walk with him.

"You had consistently high references from Mem Gesevich, much higher than most, you know. Don't be upset by Mon Draper's questioning your qualifications—I think he merely wanted the prestige of being overlord for the glass garden as well as the classroom."

"He's my teacher—he has a right to an opinion," said Ella, although his presence had irritated her.

Then, coming around a corner at full tilt, Mart and Sorb on their way back to the compound for lunch.

They looked like a pair of little boys, their mouths open as if their adenoids were swollen, eyes riveted, wrists and shoulders and hips caught awkwardly out of motion sequence for just an instant, and then even more awkwardly slamming back into the broken rhythm.

"I'll leave you now," said Elder Saint Gabriel. "I expect you'd prefer to talk alone." Serene as an old monk, he pattered away without a backward glance. Ella, in the miserable wake of his passage, almost wished he hadn't left her.

"Tell us what now," said Mart in a steely voice.

Sorb could only stare, and twist the shiny hair at the nape of his neck around his little finger.

By the time she got to the glass garden, she felt she'd gone three days without food or drink. Mart had been furious with her for accepting the responsibility of running the glass garden, and scornful of her new title. "Well, of course it's ridiculous," she'd cried, "but it was going to happen anyway; it might as well have happened now. And someone has to take care of the kids, and better me than another!"

Mart had said, "They've got you. They've swallowed you up as if you were a piece of candy. And you're just persuading *me* to be careful of being— yeah, colonized. You've been colonized yourself, you idiot. You'll start being prim, polite. It's revolting. Next thing you know you'll be preaching docility and silence. . . ."

"You don't really know me at all, do you?" she said. "As if I would! I made my pitch for immunity from j-guards, and won. Don't think I've stopped fighting."

"Are you proud of this appointment?"

"Yes. In a way. Well, why not?" She was telling the truth. She had always imagined this role; she loved the children. In a world where day became night only by the programmed reduction of electric light, change and drama and ritual had a more potent wallop than anything else. And children were at the heart of all that. It was awful, it was frightening, she didn't want to be fully a woman yet. But it was strange and exciting, and it did make her proud.

Sorb, gentle Sorb, had said, "Well, if we can mess up the reputation of one mem we might as well go for broke," and he had kissed her lightly on the cheek, with a weak but heartening warmth that seemed like the old Sorb. She had put her arms around him and missed him more than ever. Come back, Sorb. We need you. I need you. Mart is too harsh and you were my friend. I'm waiting.

In Mem Gesevich's record module Ella found plans

172

for the afternoon's activities. Lunch, exercise, toilet, quiet time, story time, choice time, snack time, exercise, song time. If only she'd had a day or two to prepare. But right on schedule the children began to arrive. Sam and Abe Mbulu. Tachi X'an. Baby Andrew Afshar. Charles Trualt in his oversize wheelchair. The Ackerholm twins, Glenda and Belinda.

As they had their lunch, Ella watched them and tried not to interfere too much. Let them get used to her new authority slowly. Now she was glad for that time, a while ago, when Mem Gesevich had been sick; the kids had some experience with Ella's being in charge.

They didn't want to talk to her at first. So she just took in, gratefully, the full small clean paleness of them. Their runny noses and twisting fingers, their hair all shot through with static electricity spiking and furrowing it. Their over sensuous eyelashes, and that blameless animal expression. The inkspot punch of their dark pupils. The soft bluntness of chins, as if they'd been rubbed for aeons by tides and coastal winds. The wiseness of their expressions, however misleading, which stayed with them until about the age of eight, when defensiveness and cleverness took over and the look of wisdom was lost or carefully hidden. Or merely reserved for six or seven decades.

She was their teacher now. Mem Mencken. They'd have to learn it.

But before she began the effort to teach them that, she took the kids to the toilets. First things first.

They lined up, and one by one had their buttons,

snaps, zippers, and clasps undone for them, and one by one requested help in being wiped or in pushing the soap releaser, and one by one emerged from the toilet full of new rocket-fuel energy. All except Charles, who managed by himself.

Then, back in the glass garden, Ella broke routine for the first time by allowing them to race around in a chain, with outstretched arms dipping left, then right, following the lead of crazy Abe. They played Duck Duck Goose and Here We Go 'Round the Mulberry Bush. Ella prepared puzzles, jignets, and corner cubes on a central table. Throughout, she wondered if Mem Gesevich's old expression of skeptical strength had surfaced at all on her own face today, or when, if ever, it would.

At puzzle time, as the chattering fell to a quiet nonsensical syllabling of mental effort, Ella sat next to Charles Trualt and helped him fit his jignet on the spokes. His arms were strong, but small-muscle coordination often let him down. Ella held the rods and strings and followed his instructions.

"Mem Gessy's dead and you're the boss," he observed.

"Yes." She felt herself come forward a little bit, not physically, but in her attitude, as if a curious primitive creature inside her had been tempted toward the spectacle of the metaphysical pondering of Charles Trualt. Charles, with his shriveled forearms even more twisted in thought, his deep-sunk eyes—suggesting cleverness, doubt, trust, all at once.

"Is it true we might get out of here someday?" he said.

174

She was startled by his shift of topic. "Of course it is." She tugged at the shoulders of her tunic and thought of the problem of being honest at all times. "That is, it might be true. It could be."

Charles sighed. "I wonder sometimes if it's just an idea everybody had, and there isn't really any possibility of Groundhog Day—"

"Charles Trualt, you stop that right now." She kept her voice low so as not to alarm the others. "That's the kind of thought that gets you in trouble. I was born and brought up above ground and I remember a lot of things about it. You just have to trust that I'm telling you the truth."

He looked at her a minute with a stare that reminded her of a camera lens. *Don't look like a machine at me, Charles*, she thought. *Look like a child.*

"It seems to me it's time for rest period," he said, as if by way of apology.

"Thanks. You're right." She smiled at him for a short moment, and turned her gaze away. Suddenly her eyes were shot through with tears, and her lashes gummy and her nose hot and itchy. Her primitive had run back into its jungle orchards to whisper the news of Charles Trualt's assumption: that all of this metallic comfortable colony was the only reality left, and up above was simply an idea. Something to carry them on from day to day, to feed their hopes and tame their angers. The history of the millennia had brought the world to this: a handful of accursed survivors trying to believe that the past had happened and that the future was possible. And she was now a mem, and

175

the new revolutionary was a partly paralyzed child in a wheelchair, taking her place.

Deep in the chiller Mem Gesevich's neurons were being frozen, and the dream of the above-ground world was being crushed and pressed by nevron gas out of her sorry mottled skull with its salmon sprigs of hair. Whether it would be true or not for Charles Trualt, the above-ground world had been no more than a hope for Mem Gorpa Gesevich. She had tried to keep the children safe from despair. She had tried to put herself between them and the blankness of the future. . . .

Now, as Ella bit her lip to bring things back under control, all of the wrong things happened, in that rebellious way that bodies assert their superiority over minds. Her eyes stung and the tears rolled. Her vision clouded, she had to touch a desk to keep her balance. Worst of all, a throaty phlegmy gasp escaped her. The children whom she had been charged to protect—not by the Elders, no, no, but by Mem Gesevich—the children who were her own dream of the future turned and saw her standing like a nincompoop in the center of the glass garden, bawling louder than they could.

21/Devil's Delight

A couple of days before E-Day, Mem Wonski took
Sorb aside in her little office. Bitter orange wall lights
stung his eyes, and a master scanner went blipping
away in a high-strung manner. Mem Wonski treated
Sorb to a long harangue that seemed both apologetic
and accusatory. At the end of it Mem Wonski told him
she was certain they'd see a lot of each other here and
there. He decided he'd been told that he was out of a
job.

She was looking away as he got up to leave the
room. There seemed to be something more that
needed to be said. He settled his eyes on her for a
minute or two as if the mere sight of her would bring
back his old intuition about people and the taking care
of them.

Her eyelashes were long and dainty, far more
lovely than the rest of her work-hardened expression.
Her hands tapped a code of impatience and stress
against her forearms.

"You know, I don't hold any grudges against you for what you've done," he said at last.

"What I've done!" She bristled.

"The lisopress treatment. And all."

"You did that to yourself, Sorb Vavilys, and don't you go high-handing me the lousy fallout of it. You were your own enemy in that, and I only followed the guidelines set down by the Elders. *They* made the recommendation, you know. You know that, don't you? Nothing as—no lisopress treatment can be given just by someone's say-so. I resent the implication. It's just another reason why you're being removed from this slot. I can't say I've made any suggestions about your next assignment, either. Frankly, I'm not sure if you're qualified any longer—"

"It's okay," he told her. "I don't even care."

He left in the silence that followed, picked up the small pouch of personal items at his console, and bid the backs of his colleagues good-bye with a small wave that none of them saw.

Back at Jefferson, he offered to help Mon Troy and Mem Nazira prepare dinner. "You're early, Sorb," noted Mem Nazira, but that was as far as her observations went. So Sorb shredded acemyte into a bowl and mixed in a dressing of everoil and vinegreen, and let his fingers get soft and slick with the work.

He didn't mind being let go. Mem Wonski had never liked him. But the thought of having nothing to do gave him a sore stomach.

The voice of the ghost was speaking, but he couldn't make out the words.

178

Images of the Dead kept coming to him out of nowhere, flapping like flags in a Gulf Stream wind. It was like a police lineup. His friends and his family kept stepping forward, one by one, hesitant and a little embarrassed, to offer themselves as the possible possessor of the ghost voice. But with infinite reluctance, he had to admit that none of them matched. And their fading away was then a mournful act. It was as if he were dooming them to a second death.

Still, while they moved and rippled in his mind, visually distinct only when he didn't concentrate on them closely, he enjoyed their presence. It was a refreshing change from the static society of the Pioneer. Daddy, with the carmite-pinned hip still causing him to wince every time he forgot and let his weight settle on that side. And his striped plainweave shirts from the shops outside Saloniki. That long concrete waterfront in Saloniki, with the sea making its baby noise: notice me, notice me, notice me, in and out all day and all night.

Mommy. She never stayed in one place in his recollections—she was always in motion. Boston, Washington, Manila. Running to catch trains, or the low shuttles, or the long high transoceanic jets. Always in a business suit, always a briefcase, always a steady hand for the soul on board who fell ill. Lavishing presents from the Manila cousins: more barongs than anyone knew what to do with.

The calmer days, when a family could hope for a life together.

"You're turning that into meal, Sorb. Don't work it

179

over or we'll have to eat it with spoons," said Mem Nazira. "Wash your hands and lay the table."

He did as he was told.

Ella came in and was grumpy, throwing some administrative forms on the bed in her cubicle, disappearing for a shower before supper. She had too much to do now, while he had too little. She had stepped forth and become a mem and taken charge of the glass garden; strange, that. It made him feel odd, as if someone were touching an exposed nerve in his neck with a scrap of tarnished silver.

He was proud of her, of course; he reminded himself that. But somewhere out of sight the friendship between them had run and was hiding, and though he whistled for it and pretended not to notice it was gone so it might sneak back of its own accord, it just didn't return.

He saw her come back from her shower with her hair slicked down in uncharacteristic neatness. He opened his mouth to say something and she beat him to it, with "Don't make any smart comments tonight, Sorb, I'm just not up for it."

Mem Dora came in, and she and Ella went into her cubicle. Ella had her hand-drawn music paper with her. It must be another lesson in composition or something.

Mem Waterhouse noticed that too, and remarked that today was no day to be engaged in the pursuit of trivial pleasures.

"Why, what day is it?" said Margaret, turning from her place at the table where she was playing with the baby's doll, and, intermittently, with the baby.

180

"By the old calendar," said Mem Waterhouse, "it's Good Friday."

"What's so good about it?"

"It's the day our savior died on the cross for us."

"Lemme outa here," said Margaret. "Don't sound good to me."

"We have to have Good Friday before we can have Easter Sunday."

"E-Day, E-Day," said Margaret, "that's all we ever get around here is E-Day. Somebody ought to be shot."

"Oh, if you were my child—"

"My name would be Margaret Waterhouse."

Mem Waterhouse snapped her fingers as if to generate heat for her hands. Then she turned and went into her cubicle and shut the door forcefully.

"Oh, everybody's in a good mood, I can see that," said Mem Lotus, coming in and dropping the compound's ration of milk substitute on the counter. "Margaret's got her favorite pout on, Sorb is mooning again, and three of the cubicle doors are closed. What've you been doing, Mem Nazira, chopping stingonions?"

"Don't blame me, Mem Lotus."

"Ahhhh." She slipped her outer tunic off and shook it once, and folded it into a little square. "The devil's wife fed him cold oatmeal this morning. He's mad at her and won't go home for supper. He's visiting us instead."

"Where?" said Margaret.

"La la la, here there and everywhere." Mem Lotus

slipped her old shoes off and stood on one foot, vigorously massaging the instep of the other. "He got in my shoes this afternoon and sent pains shooting right up my legs."

Margaret inspected the shoes. "Gone now."

"I wish."

Sorb finished laying the table and thought about the devil. If today really was Good Friday—at least by someone's reckoning—the devil probably was abroad, in a foul mood, prodding people into nastiness, even evil. Murder, brutality, betrayal, jealousy. He should take care not to be infected.

Human disintegration was like a beloved dessert to a devil's meal. Devil's delight. The slower, the more banal, the better.

Maybe it was the devil who had caused Mem Wonski to tell him he couldn't come back.

At supper he managed to get a seat next to Ella.

She was beautiful, was the problem, was the solution too. She had the softest of cheeks—they bulged out from the lower lashes in an urgent curve, like the top of a good old-fashioned apple. And like an apple, they had the pinkest of undertones behind the sturdier varnish. The tucks of skin at the ends of her smile were just right, crimped just so; she was a notch or two this side of being a pouter. The froth of hair—dark as country midnights, but shining like stars too—set her face off with theatrical intensity. Was it possible to sit next to someone so lovely and just keep shoving the acemyte salad in your mouth?

182

She caught him staring for a moment and said lightly, "You have a good afternoon, Sorb?"

"Nah," he said, gripping at common logic, trying to shove off the tidal-wave ravages of feeling that so often now set him apart. "Not particularly a good afternoon. I'm headed from bad to worse, I think."

She put two fingers on the edge of the table and her arms went close to her side as if holding herself in. "Oh? How's that?"

"Oh, I don't want to say here—"

She glanced around. "They're all busy. What is it?"

"Mem Wonski told me I was off maintenance lab duty now."

"Oh. Well you weren't exactly fond of her."

"No. But I think I'm being taken off all duties now. She didn't mention a replacement assignment, and you know that's how they usually do it."

"All duties? Sorb, that's not likely."

"That's the picture I got."

"Well, she must be giving the wrong picture. There's too much to be done for you to be—but oh, Sorb, what a blow." She was looking at him directly now, as she used to before the world went awry and noisy. "There isn't any need for that." She put her hand under the table and felt for his.

Her fingers burrowed into his clenched hand, and the feeling of them urged a warmth into his palm and fingers. Her hand twisted then and caught his in a grip less romantic than consoling, the handshake of old beloved friends. Here they were, only fifteen, and they'd lived through what seemed a whole lifetime of sturdy friendship.

What would have been passion, in a random sampling of Sorb's daydreams and nightstreams, had already aged, unnaturally, into loyalty and low-simmering affection.

He withdrew his hand from hers.

While Mem Waterhouse and Mem Nazira were clearing the table, Ella went aside with Elder Saint Gabriel. Sorb took Margaret on his lap and tried to make her sing, but she was in a cantankerous mood and pulled away. The others got out the worn old playing cards and began a game of Slip My Slipper, dealing the antique cards with care, because when they were gone there would be no others.

Elder Saint Gabriel's voice stayed low and measured, but Ella's voice penetrated. Sorb felt his stomach tighten itself as if for a punch. "It seems to me it's a question of protocol. If you can't answer this question you can at least tell me who can. That's your job as an Elder, isn't it?"

"Mem Ella, temper," said Mem Lotus. "Your blood pressure, dear. Your face is as red as a cranberry."

"I'm asking a simple question. Can I have a simple answer or not?"

Mem Dora, who was setting dishes in the heat trays for cleaning, called from her place, "Mem Ella, is this a public matter?"

"Yes, it is. At least it should be."

Everyone looked at her. Elder Saint Gabriel shook his head slightly and tried to hide a smile. "My word, we've loosed a sharp-tongued—"

"The question is: Who has the right to remove a person from assignment?"

Sorb's stomach received the punch. He caught his bile by sheer willpower, making those internal systems turn to steel just by his word to them.

"Mem Ella knows quite well that the Council of Elders assigns positions—"

"I mean remove someone from a position *permanently*. Without reassigning them to anything. Who makes that decision?"

The silence in the compound was proof that the question had its captivating side.

"The question, Ella, should be addressed by Sorb to the Council of Elders when they're in session tomorrow."

"Oh, come on," snapped Ella.

"Don't, Ella, it's okay," said Sorb.

"It's not okay," she said. "You're not going to be pushed around as if you had a hole in your head. I want to know."

"Let me decide. It's my issue. And I don't care, okay, so leave it alone."

"Sorb, Sorb," said Mem Lotus. "It's all right, Sorb." She came to him and nearly suffocated him with her lemonwater scent; she pulled his head to her side as if it were a bottle whose stubborn lid she was trying to loosen. "Don't be bothered by the

185

workings of this deal. It's just everyday business, that's all."

He was sniffling. His face was wet. How mortifying.

"Look at that," said Ella, and then seemed to lose momentum for a minute. But she turned back to Elder Saint Gabriel and said, "Hysterics don't answer the question, and I want it answered. I deserve an answer. I demand it."

"And," said Mem Dora, "she should get one, too, I think."

Elder Saint Gabriel had always treated Mem Dora with a quiet but respectful attitude. But now his placid expression wrinkled into an uncharacteristic frown—nearly a sneer, if Sorb could trust his eyes. "Again the underdog gets your vote, Dora Prite—it's a wonder you haven't been run out of town on a rail, or some similar fate, with the underdogs you've befriended."

Sorb noticed the great insult of Elder Saint Gabriel's denying the proper title for Mem Dora—only in intimate love or rank venom did such occur—and the room fell silent, until Mem Dora dropped a dish she was holding and it ran in circles on the floor, settling finally with a metallic clip.

"The question hasn't been answered yet, Elder Saint Gabriel," she eventually said.

"In the interest of camaraderie in the compound, please, answer it!" said Mem Troy. "My head, it's pounding like nobody's business."

Elder Saint Gabriel said, "It's my understanding

186

that in very severe situations, under the recommendations of a work supervisor or an Elder, the Council of Elders may act at their own discretion and decide that the work assignments of a member of the support force can be changed. Or dropped completely."

"So it's you who did this," said Ella.

"A full vote of the acting Council of Elders accomplishes this. I wasn't voting today—I was on exercise—"

Ella turned and left the common area, fuming. Mem Dora followed her into her cubicle. Margaret tried to gain admission as well and was denied, and stood glowering outside the door at the whole lot of them.

"Sorb. My apologies," said Elder Saint Gabriel. "Clearly, you're upset. I am assuming that Mem Wonski did a poor job of informing you of the reasons. It isn't my intention to do so publicly, but if you come to the Council Room tomorrow, I will help you get a reasonable explanation. You have a very loyal friend in Mem Ella, you know that."

Maybe. Maybe. But the temporary lucidity brought back by Ella's beauty was pulling away now, and the terror of her newfound temper impressed upon him the great differences between them. He was falling, tumbling out of the orbit he'd lived in so long—weeping in public, being dismissed from his job, being pitied by his best friends—and Ella was climbing ever higher toward power and pride. They were passing each other, and he might fall too far, and crash, a useless mash of words, dreams, and a former life. He might be just a shell, like the shell Ella wore around her neck, and inside it would be only one sound repeating forever: the sound of that threatening voice saying *Sorb, Sorb, Sorb.*

22/ E-Day

Mart was attending the E-Day service because he was bored and Agnes Treasure was giving him a headache. Thirty people had gathered in the gallery, to listen to readings and dizzy meditations. Mem Waterhouse sat bolt upright in front with her Bible, anticipating her turn to read. The old acemyte harvester, Mem Bettina, turned and gave him a wink. Mem Troy waddled in and found a seat near the back. Mon Micklersohn, Elder Fitchell, Mem Mbulu. Others—and then at the last minute, Ella herself, slipping into a chair behind a steel girder.

Mem Ella.

As Elder Fitchell stood to welcome everyone, Mart left his seat and moved around behind the crowd to where Ella had placed herself. When Elder Fitchell began a reading about the creation of the world, Mart arrived, reaching out to squeeze Ella's hand before she'd a chance to pull away.

"What're you doing here, you old sinner?" he whispered.

"Shh. What're you?"

"Bored to death."

"Me too."

A man behind them tapped Ella's chair with a hard finger. So they fell silent and listened to the story of God's love affair with Himself, giving Himself more and more elaborate presents and seeing that they were good. Mart thought the story showed God to be lacking in a certain amount of native intelligence. If He couldn't see that the grand finale—the creation of man and woman—was less than good, was in fact disastrous—"And God looked at what He had created and saw that He had made a serious mistake"—then He probably deserved the elaborate turning away from Him that the Jews and Gentiles persisted in doing throughout the millennia. A child eventually gets a sour taste in the mouth when the failings of the parents become evident.

Then there were readings about Noah and the new covenant, about the escape from Egypt with the horse and his rider being cast into the sea, and other splashy events. It really wasn't too bad if you didn't take it seriously. Mart could see Mem Waterhouse up there elevated in transports of devotion with every passing story. When she stood to read, her voice broke several times and it was clear she was on the edge of tears. Such a hard-nosed person, and brought to public embarrassment by stories in a book.

Despite himself, then, for a minute or two, he felt

sorry for her. She wasn't anybody's special friend in Pioneer. He'd watched her compound mates treating her with steady dignity but nothing approaching warmth or genuine affection. She was just another kind of casualty in the melee, and for the one day a year she had the attention of people, she could hardly stand up under it.

Such small things that kept people going.

What was it that kept him going? Or Ella?

Or now, his job swept away from him, Sorb? Would *anything* keep him going?

Afterward there was a wonderful leisure of holiday in the air. People stood around chatting about the service, about E-Days past. Mem Bettina went from here to there and said in a cordial old-fashioned way, "Happy Easter to you," to each person. When she came to Mart she said, "Happy Easter to you, Mart Rengage, and watch your step."

"I'm surprised you remember my name."

"Do you hear me?" she said. "I say watch your step."

"What do you mean?"

"That j-guard that is goading you that day comes back and asks us all sorts of questions after you go. He wants to know if you are seen tinkering around with the mechanical lock systems. He's out to get some facts on you, Mart, and he has that kind of look, it makes me nervous."

Ella came up just then, and Mem Bettina turned away, saying, "I don't know what you do, what you

don't do. But you better do it careful. Mon Conway's
brex-wrench and all. Just you be—"

He grabbed her arm and she winced. "Sorry," he
said softly, "sorry about that. What do you mean,
Mon Conway's brex-wrench?"

She eyed Ella, who seemed alarmed at his sudden
enthusiasm. Mart said, "It's all right, she's a friend.
What about the brex-wrench?"

"He brings one out and asks each of us if we ever
see you with one. I never see one of those things
before or since. And so I tell him. So I don't care if you
got one or you don't got one, just you be—"

Ella said, "Don't squeeze her arm, Mart. You're
hurting her."

"Sorry. Did he have any other tools with him?"

"That is that. No more." She rubbed her forearm.
"I need to go now. Don't take me so serious. I am
most likely not knowing what I say." She moved
slowly along, continuing her Easter greetings.

"Did you hear that?" He was elated, and tried to
keep his voice down. He scooped up Ella's hands in
his, for an instant, and then dropped them in case
anyone was watching. "Let's go up to an amity room.
I want to talk to you."

"I've promised Mem Dora I'd be back before too
long. It's our lesson this afternoon—"

"Oh, come *on*," he said. "Let Mem Dora take care
of Margaret for a change instead of hoarding you."
He started to drift out of the gallery, and Ella allowed
herself to be tugged along.

In an amity room, with the door closed, and a comfortable position accomplished, and some medicinal affection applied to their formal and awkward friendship, Mart said, "Do you know what that was all about?"

"Obviously I don't."

"I think it means that Mon Conway has lifted a brex-wrench from wherever they're stored and locked. That's one of the universal tools needed to open the hatch. I know it positively absolutely, within an inch of my life. Nobody's supposed to have them. He must suspect me of trying to break out of Pioneer entirely, and he thinks I've smuggled one in myself, or built one, or some other such impossibility."

"I didn't know he had such a thing against you."

"Well. I guess I didn't either. But I think it's the difference between being a kid and an anointed adult; I think it gets to you. I'm coming around to your theory, Ella, that there's something not normal about how people cower without seeming to cower about how they're sucked into the whole *idea* of how they're supposed to be here. I think that's what's happened to Mon Conway. I think you better be care ful it doesn't happen to you."

"Well. Maybe it doesn't happen to everyone, not all the way," said Ella. "Mem Dora has her way of being herself. And didn't that old woman just take the time to warn you that Mon Conway was out to get you?"

"You've got me hooked on this now, and I'm not stopping," said Mart. "You've just got to find out more about Mem Dora. So we can know how much she's changed. Who can you ask? Let that be your chore. I'm going to see if I can steal that brex-wrench from Mon Conway before he sneaks it back to where he took it from. He'll be so liable to get in a snagload of trouble if they discover it's missing and they trace it to him!"

"That's a pretty nasty thought."

"He's going around asking questions about me, trying to prove me traitorous? That's not nasty? I'm only playing by the new rules, Ella."

When Ella arrived back at Jefferson, only Mem Dora was there. "They all went to the gallery. The choir is going to sing. They thought you'd want to join them to hear it," said Mem Dora.

"No, I don't," said Ella.

Mem Dora smiled. "Your lesson is more important."

"Well, yes, it is," said Ella, "but I thought we could talk some instead of having a lesson—"

Mem Dora relaxed her smile. "Don't stretch an inch into a mile—"

"I'm a mem now," said Ella, "and I can't be lectured in the same way as before."

"Well, yes. True enough."

"When I went before the Council of Elders yesterday, and tried to get some answer about why Sorb had had his job taken away, they wouldn't talk to me. But outside the room, Elder Saint Gabriel chatted with me for a moment, and I asked him what he meant when he said it was a wonder you hadn't been run out of town on a rail."

Mem Dora said calmly, "You shouldn't have asked that. What did he say, Ella?"

"It's *Mem* Ella," she said with a sniff. "What do you think? Of course he didn't answer me."

Mem Dora brought the opposite fingers of her hands together with solemnity. She still looks like a star, Ella thought, but she's an ordinary woman with an ordinary history, and I can hear it now. "Tell me," she said, somewhat scornful of the power in her voice but willing to live with it, yes indeed.

"Oh, well," said Mem Dora at last, "let's make this quick."

"Okay by me."

"What do you know of me?" said Mem Dora, "except that I'm a crabby proud old soul?"

"You were a singer," said Ella, "but that's all I know."

"Let me spare you the family background, then, how I got from being Dolores San Agustino to Dora Prite—it doesn't really come into it. All you need to know is that near the beginning of my career I met Mon John Prite, whom I eventually married. You know that much? And John was—"

"What did you sing? How did you begin your career?"

"I was with Mem Ruby Prendergast and her band in Paris. I did the full range—torch songs, gospel rags, space salvos, baroque arias. You name it. Lieder, lullabies, whatever. A crazy quilt, really. Mem Ruby was always after me to specialize. So I met John and—"

"How did you get your title? The Morning Star?"

"Oh, that nonsense." Mem Dora looked pleased to be interrupted about this. "It's a tag-on line to that old nineteenth-century song called 'Shoo, Fly, Don't Bother Me.' A song that has its own weird history. There's that silly verse, 'I think I hear the angels sing, I think I hear the angels sing, I think I hear the angels sing, The angels now are on the wing,' and then a lovely little bit, 'I feel, I feel, I feel, I feel like the morning star.' And it repeats. That song became my signature tune, for some strange reason, and the Morning Star stuck. You know media people, they love to make you up as a deity."

Ella, testing her new authority as a mem, said, "Sing it."

"I'm trying to tell you about my husband," said Mem Dora sharply, "so let me. I met him in Paris, at the start of my career, and later married him. He was just beginning a political career in the diplomatic corps—later went on to become a senator from the state of Maine. I was singing all over the place, and had Margaret—this was six years ago now. John was a leader in the fight against the space police policy— you wouldn't have been paying attention to that battle, you were too small.

"I went along with John and sang at the rallies against the preparations for war that were going on at the time. I never spoke, just sang. Mass meetings, in Central Park, in Irrigation Springs, Nevada, on the waterfronts in Boston urb and Miami urb and in Lincoln Park in Chicago urb. That was when the big push

196

for underground shelters was made by Washington—as if all the people of North America, to say nothing of the rest of the world, could be crammed into bunkers underground. Sheer lunacy.

"So John was arrested on trumped-up charges. Two months later he died in prison."

Ella stared beyond Mem Dora, at the old faded scenery of the Grand Canyon. She didn't move a muscle.

"I was pregnant with Mazerius at the time, and when he was born, I kept on singing—mostly against the false promise of the colonies. You should have seen the media blitz advertising the things! 'Every comfort!' Stocked with impossible luxuries. Presenting a fake sense of security. . . .

"Anyway, there we were, standing before a marauding crazed bull elephant thinking that our mosquito repellent was going to protect us. And a week before the blasts—those crazy bombs in Boston, and Lord knows where else, probably the whole world over—Mazerius was kidnapped from me after an outdoor rally. He was a babe, in a tiny corduroy papoose. . . . Well, I'd become a symbol of protest, you see, a spokesperson—or songsperson. But when the warnings came, Margaret and I were carted here against our will and stuffed down here, to survive in the very prison which John and I fought so hard against. And who knows how many millions have died. Maybe everyone."

Ella turned her face to the wall. *Everyone* meant the little baby in the corduroy papoose, too.

"Do you know what I'm saying? Do you hear me? I was kidnapped, Mem Ella, and incarcerated here, when I'd rather have died up above with my baby, with all the other millions of people who must've died in the A-Day attack. The people in power thought they could make a political point by having me here, thought they could point to me and say, 'Look, she preaches against it but she's the first one inside when danger looms.' Unfortunately, the millions they might have hoped to pass that message along to never lived to hear it. So who could be surprised that people here detest me and resent me? I'm the only one here who didn't want to come, and I'm taking up room that someone else could have had. I'd resent me, too."

After a while, Mem Dora said, "Have I been too rough in the telling? Forgive me, Mem Ella. You asked, after all."

"Yes," said Ella, "I did ask."

23/ The Silence of the Morning Star

In the neglected stairwell to which she'd gone before, Ella found refuge again.

The story of Mem Dora Prite was both clearer and murkier now. She *had* had a life, she *had* spoken out—she had sung out!—for something important. Her baby had been left behind, her older child buried with her in the safety vault she'd been protesting. The irony of it was enough to choke you. No wonder Mem Dora kept such a cold face, kept her past out of the hands of others. Everyone here must know it anyway. It was why people bad-mouthed her all the time.

But she'd done little to maintain her reputation as a protester since Ella had known her in Pioneer. She'd never sung. She'd never mounted a campaign against the Council of Elders. The only time she made a serious fuss was when she stepped in to provide an alibi for Mart and Sorb.

How could she change so much? Was it losing her

baby? Was that it? Mem Dora had said very little about that part of the story, and Ella, scarcely believing what she was hearing, didn't feel in a position to ask questions. Her throat wasn't working, anyway.

Maybe Mem Dora wasn't the powerhouse Ella had always imagined.

She was still beautiful. Her words were moving, her story simple and convincing. But no matter what battles she'd fought in the past, the cold horror of the truth was that she had given up. Or was that the truth?

Mem Dora's face glowing in her memory, Ella sat still and tearlessly mourned, as if she were about to get up and go back to Jefferson Compound and find that Mem Dora had died. There was no way to swallow down the grief of the past, of the calcifying present, of the voice like a morning star that would no longer sing.

24/ Second Darkness

Mem Lotus was a tree of purple silk with gold thread stitched through it. Her arms went out on both sides; she looked like a gaudy scarecrow for a Japanese emperor.

"Happy E-Day! I love the holidays despite my religious amnesia. Any chance to dress up."

"You're gorgeous," said Sorb.

"You look like a big colorful moth about to be pinned to a piece of cardboard," said Mart, who had just stopped by.

"Would that we had lamb for dinner tonight, and lemon, and mint sauce, and potatoes baked with paprika," Mem Lotus gushed. The others hushed her; wishing out loud was thought uncourteous.

"You're lovely—can I stay for supper?" said Mart.

"Flatterer. Yes."

Sorb expected Mart to hang around Ella's chair, but to his surprise Mart squeezed in next to him and threw his arm across his shoulder and said, "Happy E-Day, Sorb," and gave him a kiss. "Happy E-Day, everybody."

Mart in a good mood made everybody wary.

"Here, take some of my meal; I'm not hungry," said Ella. She passed her plate, and the others added to it as it went around the table. Mart began to chatter and tell funny stories about the afternoon in Lincoln Compound. The life of the party, as Sorb sat still and beleaguered by the voice inside him.

"Sorb, you got a while before Episode, come on out with me, why not?" said Mart when the conversation got noisy.

Sorb picked up his knife and balanced it at the fulcrum between his thumb and forefinger. A line of text from his studies with Mon Draper came out of nowhere to him, about the development of the human fetus. "In the twentieth week, the thumb can oppose the fingers."

Mart ignored that, and by dint of his blond gravity pulled Sorb, somewhat against his will, from the E-Day supper table and out of the compound, where Mart set up a rolling pace.

Mart said he thought they'd walk over to Lindenhurst Compound and play a trick on foxy Mon Conway. See if there could be a way for Sorb to sneak in his cubicle and do a snatch-and-run. Looking for a lightweight tool about the size of a five-year-old's forearm, and shaped much the same, with a nodulated sensor-priser at the end. Could be under the pillow, under the cot, stuffed in the one drawer behind some

202

clothes. All for fun, of course, a lark; and Sorb would have to move quickly as a bird. Stuff the thing—the brex-wrench, it was called—into his tunic. Sorb could do that, sure? Sure he could manage it, why not? Couldn't he?

Well, there wasn't any reason why not, not that Sorb could see.

Of course he'd have to be *very* careful. And they wouldn't even try to pull it off unless it seemed foolproof. Mart would give the signal. He'd wink at Sorb. Sorb would remember the signal? A wink.

They stopped in a shadowy recess and practiced.

Mart winked. It went like a thunderclap across Sorb's thoughts. Mart's lashes lowered with colossal intention, shielding acre by acre the vast taut shimmering dome of storm-gray iris, crashing and meshing and threshing with the windscreen of the lower lashes, and then coming to an interminable midpoint of lockout (when the sun and stars and moon and any other heavenly bodies up there were sure to have fizzled and fallen due to lack of human adoration and human longing, for when the sky has been forgotten then gods yawn and orbits lose their elastic strength and the whole mesmorama slips its gears) but then like the first wave in the first ocean, the top lashes stirred and lifted and the globe of power reasserted itself, the streaks and trails of dawn dust in the revealed iris shocking him, the screws and grommets of the muscles at either end of the eye's bulge wrinkling clockwise and back again, and finally Sorb was naked as a fish before the eye of a whale, about to be eaten, digested, and eliminated without the consciousness of the whale even so much as flinching. Oh you Mart. And you think I don't know anything.

"Got it?" said Mart.

"Right," said Sorb. "A wink."

But in the fear of attack by a casual wink of Mart's, or because the voice inside him was so persistently loud, he missed the cue. Mart made some excuse and went away with his bad feelings poorly disguised. Mart had leaned across the table and spoken to Sorb as if he were a dog. "Stay here, Sorb. Stay. I'm going out for a bit but I'll be back. Talk to Mem—uh, Mem Andrews. She's feeling lonely with everyone gone out to the gymnastic competition. So stay. Do you hear me?"

It was impossible not to hear, and he was watching for the wink at the same time. But the winks only came in pairs—blinks—and he knew those didn't count. So he watched Mart saunter away and he turned to Mem Andrews. She was slowly dying of an internal cancer which gave her no rest. The winces were accompanied by groans, and the groans by apologies, and apologies by pauses to gasp for air, and then the winces rushed in again.

While the conversation wasn't startling, since Mem Andrews could only apologize and Sorb could barely make out a solitary thought of his own given the distraction of the uninvited voice inside him, there was a certain comfort to its predictability. Mem Andrews was dressed in Pioneer poorcloth, the cheesy yellow yardage allocated to those whose last personal garments had finally fallen to pieces. It made her skin look more green than white, and her lips sagged, cracked and silver and dry.

"Ever hear the voice of a ghost?" mused Sorb.

"Oh my," she wheezed. "Oh me oh me oh me. Ohh."

"There's a ghost in the vicinity. It's been letting me know every now and then. I don't know exactly where, though, and I don't know who. I think it's in the tunnel beyond the hatch. I think it might be the ghost of someone who got to the hatch too late. And couldn't get in."

"Oh my goodness. Forgive me. Please."

"I've been stuck with hearing it say my name over and over—it never says anything else."

"Oh. Ahh. Oh the dickens."

"Sometimes I think I can picture it, and when I close my eyes, I think of a white rag, with a solid spherical head like a globe, and trailing garments. Oh, you should see the mouth, it's crumpled in on itself like the edges of a moist old-fashioned cake—"

"Oh. Pardon."

It was good to talk to someone again. He smiled at Mem Andrews, and told her all about the ghost, and then before long Mart was back, with Margaret Prite. Little Margaret looked smug and happy.

"Margaret wanted to come for a walk," he said loudly. "Let me sit down with you for a short while, and then we'll have to get Margaret home. Margaret, you go play. That's okay, isn't it, Mem Andrews?"

She gave her assent. Mart sat down kitty-corner to

Sorb, pulling a chair up almost to Mem Andrews's lap, and leaning forward with his forearms balanced on his knees so he could stare right up into Mem Andrews's face. "Did you enjoy the E-Day goings-on?"

"Uff," she said, and made a little dismissive motion with her hand. "Fluff."

"That's what I think. But over at Sorb's they do everything fancy all the time. Mem Lotus was trying to get Mem Dora to sing again this afternoon—"

"Fiend," said Mem Andrews. "Pardon. She's wicked. She's—"

"That's not true," said Sorb. "Just quiet in her emotions. She keeps to herself—what's wrong with that?"

"Quiet in her emotions?" labored Mem Andrews. "If she hadn't fought the building of colonies— there'd be a lot more dug and occupied now—you ass. Oh, Christ."

"I don't buy all that," said Sorb.

"Sorb." Mart lifted his head a few degrees and his eyes looked up at an angle, his glance barely clearing his furrowed blond brows. "It's not a topic for conversation. I shouldn't have brought it up."

"Where'd Margaret go?" said Sorb suddenly.

Mart's fingers tightened on one another. "Oh, around." Sorb wanted to leave.

Then it happened. It was as if the room had been pinched from the rest of the lighted colony and pulled at top speed through the soil to another buried homesite, there to rest and remain alone, without the benefit of Pioneer's life support systems. Sorb felt Mart's hand reach out and grab his left knee, and the moans of Mem Andrews grew thicker and less articulate in the sudden blinding dark.

"Oh!" came the voice of Margaret, off a little way.

"Just keep on!" shouted Mart.

"I can't see!"

"Just keep on!"

"But how do you expect me to *see*?"

"Just keep on!"

"Let me go for her, Mart," said Sorb, but Mart's grasp on his knee just tightened.

"Are you okay, Mem Andrews? Don't be frightened. It's the lights—they did this once before. Have you got my hand? There, yes you have. We're all safe together here." Mart's tone was unctuous, sympathizing, but to Sorb's surprise, not entirely ironic. "I don't know what it is, but they'll go on again shortly. That's how it happened the last time."

There was a sound in the dark. Margaret's voice uttered a little curse. "Anyone who has to go hunting at a time like this—"

"Margaret," said Mart, "shut up the commentary."

Sorb had reached out and grabbed the other of Mem Andrews's hands. They sat, the three of them, touching, almost hugging each other. He couldn't believe that her yellow sackdress didn't glow in the dark. He couldn't believe that after a while his eyes weren't becoming used to the dark—able to see outlines, glints from reflective metal, cold masses and warm details. If anything, the dark was thickening around them, freezing them closer and closer together, like a black gelatin poured into the room to take the place of the empty lighted space that had existed so blithely before.

He could smell the energetic eagerness of Mart, asserting itself over his own fear, and the somewhat nose-wrinkling stench of Mem Andrews's sickness, brought up more vigorously by her quicker, anxious breathing. He tried to smell himself in the triangle but he couldn't. Mart's smell, with a soapy sweet base and a cutting touch of perspiration, and the dustiness of blond hair, was the boss smell.

"Gotcha!" said Margaret to herself, and then, "Here I come."

"Hurry up, Margaret, or the ghost will get you," said Sorb. Margaret screamed in nervous laughter.

"Shut *up*," said Mart. "Sorb, just chill it."

"Here I am," said Margaret, and her voice warned them all of her small perspiring hand which landed like a lightweight clump of dirt and dust in the middle of their juncture.

"Ah, you sweetheart," said Mart, and even in the dark Sorb could tell Mart was smiling at her. He was jealous. Glad for the dark. He winked furiously a couple of times and stuck out his tongue.

25/ Second Darkness
Elsewhere

After Mart dragged Sorb off—some new plan, some screwy plot—Ella went to her cubicle and put on her seashell, and then made her way with careful, deliberate steps through the Centrex globe. Away from Jefferson Compound, away from the horrifying story of Mem Dora.

At last, to the Council of Elders. She should have gone ages ago. Or someone should have.

They were just reconvening after their evening meal; Elder Saint Gabriel hadn't even arrived yet. Ella opened the door of the Council Room without knocking and said, "Excuse me?"

"Why, Mem Mencken," said Elder Moxie-doxie. "What a pleasant surprise."

"I would like to ask some questions," said Ella.

"Surely you can address them through Elder Saint Gabriel, your elected official?" said Elder Johnson, smiling. He continued making notes on a pad.

209

"You didn't answer me last time and I want to know," said Ella.

She was getting their attention. "Why do we still have j-guards down here?" she said. "That's question number one. Jurisdiction-guards were called up during State of Emergency way back when we were waiting for A-Day, but we've been here as peaceful as lambkins for almost five years, not so much as a peashooter to threaten us, and we're still policed like we've got hand grenades and artillery among us. Why?"

"We don't deal with complex issues like that with minors—" sniffed a man named Elder Corona.

"I'm a mem now, remember? And I asked before and was denied an answer. But I can't wait anymore for an answer."

"Don't get too big for your britches," said Elder Moxie-doxie.

"Shall I list all my questions in a row, and you can answer them in any order you want?" said Ella. Was she shouting? She never shouted. "How about Sorb Vavilys? Why was he lisopressed? Do you know what it's done to him?"

"Oh, it's that," said Elder Johnson. "The teenage heart. I might have known."

"I loved Sorb Vavilys!" said Ella. "You didn't, you didn't care enough about him to protect him from that awful lisopress. What did he do? What was his crime? Nobody knows."

"Beware overexertion, my dear," said Elder Corona.

210

"He wanted to get out of here," said Ella, "was that it? He proposed at an Episode that we ask questions of the Council, and get some public answers. So tell me, I'm asking for Sorb, since you screwed his brain up enough that he may never be able to ask questions again: Why aren't we digging our way out of here? Has anyone ever tried it? Huh?"

"We should not dignify this intrusion—" said Elder Corona, getting huffy, but Elder Saint Gabriel had just arrived, and since Ella lived in his compound, his gesture of patience was observed.

"You know as well as I do," he said, taking off his outer tunic, "that all theorists suggest that much of life on this planet has been destroyed by the bombs. You also know that there's no telling how poisoned the atmosphere is up there. Not to mention the fact that the tunnels collapsed in the explosion—"

"*I've* heard people guessing," said Ella. "They guess that maybe the world *wasn't* destroyed by A-bombs, that it was maybe a more local attack? With more conventional weapons? If the attack *wasn't* atomic, would the tunnels really be collapsed? How do I know if they really are?"

"We have no reason to lie to you, Ella," said Elder Saint Gabriel kindly. "We have nothing to gain ourselves by remaining here, except to preserve the life we've been able to salvage. It's a sacred duty. We mustn't risk it."

"Who made *you* prime judges of how to proceed?" said Ella, but she knew the answer to that.

"You did. That is, we were voted in, Ella, and you

211

know that from civics. Now we've had enough of this outburst—"

"You haven't had enough yet, because I'm not finished." She could barely believe it was herself talking like this. "Why was Mem Dora kidnapped and brought here?"

"I do object!" snapped Elder Johnson. "Ella Mencken, this is enough! We will have you removed from your post for insolence if you keep on—"

"Like Sorb!" she yelled. "Like how many other people? Who has ever suggested that we get out of here, and what's happened to them? Remember Garner Jones? Look what happened to him! That's *murder*, folks, step right up and stare it in the eye!"

It was then that the lights went out, the second time in the history of Pioneer. For a minute Ella thought she had fainted with the excitement of facing the Council of Elders, but quickly she realized what must have happened, and she yelled through the blackness, "You got systems failing and people chafing at the bit, and still you're too cowardly to open the hatch and start digging! Well I got news for you, folks. There's a word spreading in the Colony!" She was lying, but in the darkness no one could tell. "There's something being said, and it's getting louder and louder. 'Remember Garner Jones!' "

Her voice rose an octave; she was almost singing. "Remember Garner Jones!"

PART FOUR

The ghost had gotten in again, and was circulating in the draftless Upper Reaches. Sorb could sense it floating like a cloud turned on its side, like a shroud, like a small sourceless inner-lit waterfall free of context. It went past the timbers and the girders, along ramps and catwalks, down ladders and levels, through portals and grid screens.

The ghost was saying again, Sorb, Sorb, in its monotonous way, patiently drifting back and forth, here and there, and coming near to northpoint drylock. Give up, go back, Sorb said. I don't want you, I don't want to meet you, I don't care who you are or where you came from.

The ghost wafted, waiting for him.

What do you want of me?

Sorb, Sorb.

What?

Sorb, Sorb.

What is it you want?
Follow me.
Where?
Follow me.
Where?
Out.
How?
Out.
How?
Out.
How can I follow you out?
Out.
Can *we get out?*
Out.
How?
Follow me.
Who are you?
Follow me.
Who are you?
Follow me.
Who are you?
Sorb.
Who are you?
Sorb.
Who are you? Who are you, damn it?
Sorb.

26/ Further Dawn

When the lights came on again there was a dazed silence. Ella blinked twice, to reestablish the faces of the Elders in her mind, and thought suddenly: They're as scared as I am. They don't know any more than I do.

With that, she turned on her heel and left the Council Room.

Back at Jefferson Compound, Ella waited for Mart and Sorb to show up, and when they did, with Margaret in their company, Ella said, "Where were you?" with a bite and snap in her voice she didn't like but couldn't help.

Mart merely grinned and danced off to Lincoln. Margaret ran to the toilet. So Ella took Sorb's hands in hers and said, "Sorb, dear, tell me. Where'd you go?"

"We gotta get out of here," said Sorb softly.

"What is Mart doing the Cheshire Cat about?" she said. "Tell me."

"We gotta leave, Ella. Listen to me."

"Sorb Vavilys," she said, "don't go all bonkers on me when I'm asking you a serious question. I want you to answer me. Where were you and who were you with?"

"Don't yell at me," he said, unperturbed. "I *am* talking to you, so be smart enough to listen, okay?"

She said, "I'm sorry. I guess I'm jittery like everyone else. I just went through something strange myself."

"Be jittery, it doesn't matter," said Sorb. "Maybe it does some good. I got news for you, Ella. It's Easter Day. It's time to get out of here. Get out of the tomb."

She felt anger drilling against the inside of her skin, wanting to get out and hurt him. "The Elders, Sorb, are just as caught as we are here. *They* don't know any better than we do what's out there. Maybe the gossip is right, and the destruction up there *wasn't* total. But they're not going to let us find out, Sorb. They're too scared themselves."

"We're not hopeless, Ella. We can get out. We're going to."

"Sorb!" She had to keep herself from catching up his hands to her heart, because his voice was so stricken and urgent. There was a hint of the other Sorb again, that tempting glimpse that came and went every now and then, and made her remember the size of the respect she'd had for him. His dark hair was pushed back and stood up like grain in fields, bowing under the pressure of the wind. His eyes had their old needling directness. He was again, momentarily, someone she could love deeply, because at the core of his wincing smile and pleading expression was a dark hot coal: and that was mystery: and that was enough.

"You're verging on hysteria, you know that, Sorb?" She laughed lightly, and the laugh almost reversed itself in midexplosion into a teary gasp. By sheer willpower she avoided that. "Of course we're not really hopeless. Come here, sit down so they won't hear us. Nobody said we're hopeless. Look, do you want a cup of tea and larmer? It'll calm you down—"

"Forget the larmer. It's a tranquilizer. It just helps the hopeless forget their hopelessness. But we're not hopeless, I'm telling you. And we've got to get out of here. Tonight, if we can. The place is falling apart. I know we can get out. I know the tunnel isn't packed solid as they always say it is."

His face was almost glowing. "Sorb. Have you violated the confidential files?"

On his face she saw the struggle whether or not to lie. "Don't lie," she said.

"No, then, I haven't," he said. "I would only have lied because it would have made you trust me more."

"Then how do you know about the tunnel?"

"I know." He had a hard look on his face.

"You know. Great. How could we escape, even if we wanted to? There's northpoint drylock. There's the sealed hatch. Maybe there's a half a mile of rubble piled on the other side of the hatch. You're going to make three wishes and have it all disappear? Sorb, I

219

don't even want to talk about this. A sensible plan—maybe. I'm mad enough. But dreams and visions, forget it."

"Northpoint drylock is a welcome mat to us, and you know it," said Sorb. "Mart can get us through drylock with his eyes closed. And the big old hatch? Mart figured that out. It's a matter of some tools and some lead time. And he's gone and got one of the tools already."

"The brex-wrench. He didn't!"

"He sure did. Or rather, I was supposed to and couldn't quite manage, and in the end it was Margaret who actually lifted it."

"But he needs other tools."

"So we'll get them for him. There's nothing to *lose*, Ella. What is there to lose? We're going to fall down and die like Mem Gesevich some day. You want to die without seeing the sun again? We've got these hundreds of Pioneer residents here and they're all future blind. They can't think four hours ahead. It's a sickness. We're going to meet our own ghosts wandering in these halls—I mean, if we wait for a signal from above ground. Nobody's going to give us a signal, nobody's going to dig us out. We have to be the pioneers, Ella, you and me and Mart. We have to go out the way our relatives left Europe and Asia and Africa several centuries ago, and went to America, or the way they went out to the moon and Mars—we have to be the people to brave the elements. It always has to be someone and it might as well be us."

"Sorb. The tunnel."

"It's free."

"How do you know?"

He was still. She pressed. "How do you know, Sorb? Don't lie."

"I just—know it. I just know it is. It never caved in. Or if it did, it was just a small portion. You could dig through it like snow."

"You're not sure." Damn him! Her spirits had soared, and now they fell. "You have no right, Sorb, to come stirring me up. This is the purpose of larmer, you idiot; you've got a fool's dreams and you're going to ruin my emotional equilibrium here as well as yours. I want to leave as much as you, but make sense, please!"

"Ella. I've had a sign."

"What do you mean?"

"I've had a sign. I *know* this is the time to try to get out. I've been told."

"By whom?"

He wouldn't say. Twenty minutes of her best coaxing, and he still wouldn't say. Some word delivered accidentally by one of the Elders, maybe? Some scrap of conversation overheard? A printed clue spotted at some lucky moment? He was adamant. She swore that she couldn't be expected to take him seriously unless he revealed his sources. But he wouldn't.

The curfew bell rang. She said crossly, "It's nighttime and I'm going to bed, Sorb. When you have a *reasonable* escape plan, come back and tell me. That's my advice."

"You give me advice once more and I'll give you a punch in the mouth," he told her. It was so earnest a remark that she laughed, despite herself, and hurt him deeply, she could see that. So she went off to bed, chagrined.

She brought her doubts, one at a time over the next several days, to Mem Dora, disguising them as best as she could.

"Larmer? A pacifier? It might well be," said Mem Dora. "But if you go suspecting every bit of domestic minutiae as being part of a plot, you'll have a hard time resting at night."

"Sorb thinks it's why he started dreaming again— because he began to cut larmer out of his diet," said Ella.

"Makes sense to me."

Ella was annoyed. She'd wanted Mem Dora to state that it was idiotic babble. Or else to rail to the front lines, the way Ella had done at the Council of Elders. Not this even-handed restraint.

"Try the A minor scale again, please."

"But how can you not protest?" said Ella. "If you thought that the larmer was having an effect like that—pinning us 'to this awful metallic life, and never letting us think further than suppertime— You were this great protester. The Morning Star. In your day."

"And I sang then, too, and now I don't," said Mem Dora dryly. "I have my reasons."

"You're lazy. You're conceited."

222

"You're getting sassy, Mem Ella, and that doesn't mix well with musicianship. Will you try that scale?"

Another day, when Ella stepped from the shower stall and stood drying herself under the heat bars, Mem Dora and Margaret emerged from an adjacent stall and joined her. They turned gently on their squeaky wet heels, the dampness of their hair sizzling out with a slow soft crackle. Ella had learned to abandon embarrassment in the showers, because it was nearly impossible to find a time when they weren't being used or else off-limits due to curfew. As they rotated and jostled each other, cooing in the comfort of the dry heat, they were joined by Mem Wonski from the maintenance unit, who entered the shower area with her allotment of soap/shampoo in a carrying bubble. She regarded them with dim appreciation.

"And a top of the morning to you, Mem Dora, Mem Ella," said Mem Wonski. "And Margaret."

"Don't 'top-of-the-morning' me," said Ella, almost without thinking. "Not after what you did to Sorb. Forget it."

"Oh. A little snotty," said Mem Wonski. "Imitation is the sincerest form of flattery, Mem Dora; you should be impressed with such a little mimic shadowing you around."

"Come along, Mem Ella," said Mem Dora, and on the way back to the compound, said, "You're still so young, Ella. You've learned how to have an opinion but you haven't learned to put it to use yet. Don't be too hard on people."

"It's hard times," said Ella. She felt bitter. Like everyone else, she thought, you're forgetting that the lights have gone out a second time and we're that much closer to real power failure—or we might be. You're forgetting to be worried about it. You're forgetting about Sorb's suggestion that larmer is a sedative for the emotions—you're not listening. Not even you.

"Why won't you sing?" she said sadly.

Margaret had gone on ahead. Mem Dora looked at Ella as if she'd gone off her rocker. Then she sighed and said, "It's very simple, really. With Mazerius taken from me, I just don't have the heart."

"I'll find him for you. If he's still alive," said Ella, impulsively.

"Don't make it so snappy or I'll have a heart attack with the shock of it," said Mem Dora.

"Well, just tell me about it, so I know," said Ella. "If you will."

Mem Dora swung her plastic case of toiletries from hand to hand and looked straight ahead. "I told you already, most of it. It was a nightmare. I was just finishing up my encore at this rally—that lovely old complaint, 'The Tree of Life.' Maybe you never heard of it. Don't ask me to sing it, you know better. My stage manager came running right onstage screaming that the police had lifted Mazerius out of his portable bassinet and made off with him. I left immediately, tripping over the power lines looping all over the stage, pushing against the tide of cops. I scratched, I kneed, I broke someone's jaw, and I was tranquilized and carried away in a stupor. Thank God Margaret was at the home of a sitter or they'd have taken her too."

"What did you do?"

"Well, when I came to, I raised bloody hell, you can be sure. But who was to listen to me? This was the last week before the blasts. Through an old colleague of my husband's I learned that Mazerius was lodged in a state-run home for children, conveniently near one of the three model colonies. The plan was that he'd be evacuated to a colony if the need arose. A way of diffusing the force of my protests, I suppose, if it could be shown that my own child was to be protected by the very defense I was fighting against. . . . I could imagine the scenario. There'd be some minor scare, and Mazerius would be bundled off, along with lots of other photogenic children from the home, and the wind would be whipped right out of my sails. 'Heartless mother!' they'd cry. 'Wants to deny her infant son protection against the enemies!' Only it backfired on everyone, because the A-Day attack came, and there we all were. Boston blown up, I assume, and all lines of communication down. And Margaret and me dumped in here, like I said: propaganda to the end. And Mazerius? In some other colony, propaganda too? Or dead like everyone else?"

She turned to Ella. Her voice lifted to a near shout. "And you want me to *sing?* You want me to *amuse* you by singing 'Happy Birthday,' and 'Joy to the World,' and that other tripe? You will keep harping at me to sing, as if I could? As if I ever could?"

225

She looked like she wanted to hit Ella. "You can go marching boldly off to the Council of Elders, but you can't understand a whit about human beings if you keep asking me and asking me, and for crying out loud, I'm not saying it again, quit asking, quit hammering at me, just quit it, will you?"

27/An Axe to the Piano

Leaning against her in the red light of night, Ella sighed deeply. The tears were beginning to dry on her cheeks and to itch. Mem Dora's arms were folded strictly against herself now, but her breath on Ella's shoulder felt soft as dust balls.

"I have a secret," said Ella in her quietest voice. "There's a piano in the North Reaches. We could go there someday. I'm not asking you to sing—okay?—but I could play for you."

Mem Dora smiled in the dark. "You foolish child. You'll be caught one day, you know that? Caught and lisopressed. Don't go taking such risks, please. For my sake. The attack on the Council of Elders was bad enough."

"But it's not right, that piano's up there and never even been used, nobody knows—"

"I know all about that piano," said Mem Dora. "Once the Council members let me know it was there.

They wanted me to sing a concert, to prove that things were normal, that there was no dissension here in the Pioneer. I told them that I would never sing. I said I wouldn't make trouble, but I wouldn't sing. If they brought that beautiful beast near me I'd attack it with a hammer and an axe. They believed me. That would have been too much excitement."

"One thing I don't understand," said Ella. "First you were a great activist. Then you came underground and went all anonymous and blank. I can figure that much out. But what made you turn around and give an alibi for Sorb and Mart that time? You stepped out of your silence, just like that."

Mem Dora said, "Don't let me get sentimental. It's just that you had asked me about love, that time, and you'd started showing how much you could love those two. You couldn't disguise it if you tried, Ella. It was in *your* name—it was for you—that I opened my mouth. Because I was glad to see love. Because, in my own life, love seemed to have evaporated—"

"What are we going to do?" said Ella. "Not tonight—I mean for good?"

"Go back to sleep," said Mem Dora. "You'll be yourself in the morning."

Ella padded to her cubicle and closed the door. She imagined the dreams she would have—dreams of an infant child being stolen away, of music being burned, of pianos being attacked. She wanted to stay awake all night, because those images would come to her quietly in the night in dreams, and then by the morning they would have faded all away, just as Mem Dora suggested.

228

But it wasn't time to forget things anymore. *Once you can love, you can learn to act.* Mem Dora had said that several times. She'd done it herself. Ella lay in the dark, eyes wide open, remembering.

28/ Violation

It was as if Sorb himself had already gotten hold of a calibrated universal tool and was aiming it straight at his head. Mart felt giddy under the attack. Sorb and his obsession to break out were likely to smash the coherent structure of Mart's poor skull, spill his brains upon the floor.

The calibrated u-tool was far less tricky to locate than the brex-wrench. Mart knew from his own sidling around that there was a u-tool lying sweet as a sleeping puppy in a locked chamber in the systems security division. It could be seen in the glass of the locker. And since Sorb had free time—and that goofy expression that alarmed no one—it was merely a matter of getting Sorb to recognize what he must do.

Mart took Sorb aside one lunchtime.

"You don't have anything else to think about except this," he said. "Mon Dolphus carries the keys and passtones to that unit of lockers in his belt. And he's a savage until he thinks he's gotten the best of you, at which time he relaxes and lets up and tries to smooth things over. You've got to irritate him and stand up under his abuse, and then endure his apologies, too.

"He takes off his wallet-belt when he's changing from uniform to casual. You know that time. You've just got to get the keys and passtones from the wallet, work the locks, and snatch the u-tool. I can't plan it any more carefully than that. You'll be on your own. You've got to do better than you did with the brex-wrench. You were useless then."

"Oh, well."

"You can do it?"

"Sure." Sorb looked as if several midges were circling in front of his eyes; he focused on something, lost it, and said somewhat sleepily, "So what more are we going to need? Brex-wrench, u-tool, and what?"

"I'll get into the files somehow and find out some passage codes—just leave that to me."

"So you're decided."

"Hmmmmmm."

"You're decided about this now. We're going to get out, you and me."

It was hard for Mart to say. To answer Sorb, to keep him going, he said simply, "And Ella too."

"She isn't sure it can be done."

"Just *go*, Sorb, and don't mess it up or we'll all be sizzled. Don't ask me for more advice. Close your mouth. Just go and do your best. And remember we can't even *think* about getting out unless we have a u-tool. I don't care how you annoy Mon Dolphus. He's a natural brute and annoys easily. Just smile at him the wrong way. He'll probably throw a chair at you and break your head open. Go on."

Then Sorb was gone, and the delicate question reasserted itself in Mart's mind. The equation had two parts. One side was Mart's absolute disbelief in the possibility of escaping the Colony. On the other side of the equation rested the actions that Mart had gotten started and were now rolling along on their own. The clever theft of the brex-wrench (done, supposedly, for the humiliation of Mon Conway). And, once the brex-wrench was in hand, the appetite had grown for the u-tool. The digging up of the passage codes would come next. Yet what tied the two parts of the equation together? When had he been convinced that this insane game was worth playing?

He didn't know. But here he was, walking with a purpose, carefully disguised by a nothing's-up look on his face. He had an hour before afternoon assignment. Despite all the logic he could muster up, he was heading to the computer files, to see if he could dig up the passage codes.

"Afternoon, Mart," said Mem—what was her name?—from the Reagan Compound. "What's cookin'?"

"I'm on my break," he said. "I thought I'd come up and ask if I could use one of the screens."

"Sorry. You know the rules."

"Ah, I know. But the place is dead now. Everybody to lunch?"

232

"Wolfing it down. I go in a bit."

He glanced at the clock.

"What're you after? There'll be someone in to spell me when I go so don't be thinking you can sneak back in unnoticed."

"That's exactly what I was thinking." Fight with the truth if you can. "But Mem Forbush"—her name had come sailing out of nowhere—"there's just a couple of equations I want to dilly around with. I've been off-limits for weeks ever since that Mem Dora thing. My mind is itching with numbers it can't get at. It won't take long. Come on. I'll be done in a flash, I promise. Come on."

"It's on your head. You broke the rules, you pay the consequences. Mem Dora is no child of innocence and purity, you know."

"Well, neither am I."

She threw back her head and laughed. But affectionately. "Go on with you, Mart, your diapers still stink. Get lost before you get us both in trouble."

"I survive trouble."

"You, you survive Mem Dora, you can take another A-Day attack."

He had his hands on the chair before the available console. "She's a friend, Mem Forbush."

"Hello, big boy. Some friend. They used to get thrown in jail for that."

"What makes you so nasty to her?"

"She's stuck up, Mart. She's a walking ice doll. She's just another type of human being, the type that looks down on us regular Joes and Janes and won't give us the time of day. She's a miserable wretch of a mother to that girl, and you know it as well as I do. On top of that—she hasn't sung so much as do re mi since we landed here. That's a slap in the face. That smarts."

"Oh, she's not so bad." He pulled out the chair and confidently sat down in it.

"Mart, you want me to sound the alarm, or what?"

"Ten minutes. I promise." His heart was pounding like a glass thresher. He looked over and arched an eyebrow. It was his most captivating look as far as he knew. "Come on. It's worse than being sexy and no way to go. It hurts."

"Oh, you." She puffed up in exasperation and went back to her console.

Some time later she said, "Okay, party's over."

"Obedient as the weather," he sang. "Thanks so much. I won't pester you again, promise." He sailed out of the room without a backward glance, trying to close his eyes and ears to every sensory impulse so that he could remember the sequence of the passage code. Pencils and pens and paper were rare, there was nothing on which he could write what he'd just learned. He had to write it or he'd forget it. He couldn't concentrate on remembering it very hard or it would break, like a puff pastry held too tightly in the hand. Nor could he allow any interference. So with eyes almost squeezed shut, he ran down a level to the glass garden. Ella would have some tablet on which he could scribble this before it was lost. Tablets and markers went with little kids.

234

He hammered on the glass door. There was no answer. He hammered again.

"Ella," he roared, conscious of the old acemyte harvesters far away in the glass fields, turning under the torpa lamps at the sound of his voice. "Let me in. It's Mart."

The door was flung open and he pushed past Ella. "I need a piece of paper. Come on, fast, or it'll be too late." With a groan, he sensed the drain of forgetfulness opening. He wanted to put his fist in it and choke it closed. "Ella! Now!"

She was on the floor.

"Paper," said a voice, "yeah. There's some here."

All the kids were on the floor, except the one who'd spoken, who lolled regally in that oversize wheelchair. Charles Trualt, yes, he remembered him. "Where?"

"In the closet. Second shelf. Pencils above."

He broke the door open because it was locked and he didn't want to go pick Ella off the floor and go through her pockets looking for the key.

He drew the passage code out, skipping small sections which had slipped down the greedy drain, drawing lines for the spaces of the lost digits, and making the shape of it pure and true and accurate. That was it, he had it. He let himself feel splendid about having stolen the shape of the passage code, in itself a feat worthy of being recalled by his eulogizers at some point which he hoped would be in the generously distant future.

But there were five empty spaces, where the drain had won.

He fit a few digits in, to see if his memory sat up and nodded enthusiastically at recognition, but to no use. The spaces were gaping holes, like the lost teeth in the smiles of the poor old residents. The passage code was infuriating for the holes in it.

He swore softly and vigorously to himself.

"Now you should help her," said Charles.

He looked up, and saw that he'd been blind.

He helped her sit up, and he held her for a while. She sobbed and shivered and turned her face first toward him and then away. "Oh, Ella, come on, what is it?" he said. Her cheeks were shiny with tears, and her hands went up at last to rub them dry, and to rub her eyes clear. "Oh, Mart, you've no idea how awful," she said. "It was the worst nightmare. Come on, we can't leave these kids lying around on the floor."

"What happened?"

"It was Mon Conway." She reached Sam and pulled him upright. He vomited on the floor and she regretfully lowered him again. "Maybe they shouldn't be moved. Would you clean that up?"

He got some water and towels. He was horrified to see her like this, so shaken and fallen. "What did the idiot do?"

"He was having some sort of attack, Mart. He was like a lunatic. He demanded that I open the door. He said he was under emergency orders. I had no choice. He tore the place apart. He was looking for you."

"No."

"Yes, he certainly was. He went right over to the closet where you'd been hiding that last time, and he went through it, and checked the cupboards and the medicine box and behind the dressing screen. The children were in an uproar. Well, they didn't know what was going on! Mon Conway's face was blue with rage. I've never seen—and then he stopped, when he realized you weren't here, and he said, 'You're going to get it, Mem Ella Mencken. You and your pals.' And then he said, 'I'm doing a mestrol check now. And if you don't like it you can just leave.' "

"And she tried to leave," volunteered Charles, who'd been listening hard. "But he wouldn't let her take any of us with her."

"I got the Council on the diatone, and they simply said 'Approved' and hung up on me. In the meantime he grabbed Tachi and sat her down. I smacked him, Mart, but it was as if he were made of marble. His face didn't even flush. Oh, these kids—!"

"Are you all right?"

"Of course I'm all right! That's not the point!"

"I know. I'm just anxious." He reached out to her hand and she snatched it away.

"What've you done to make him so mad! And to make these kids pay like this!"

"Me? I haven't done—"

"You did too. You stole that brex-wrench. I know perfectly well you did."

He made a monster face at her and Charles Trualt said, "Oh, I can keep a secret. That's one of my hobbies."

"For a lark, Mart, for a silly joke that cost these kids! And is going to cost you plenty, too, I bet, because if he was telling the truth those j-guards are out for blood."

"But there's no proof I stole any brex-wrench."

"Oh? Where'd you hide it?"

"Wherever it is, I'm certain it's safe away."

"Oh, Mart!" Ella cast her arm out over the children. "You know what a mestrol check is like! It's *painful*! It's debilitating. *And* frightening as hell, even when you're grown up! The only reason Mem Gesevich fought the j-guards so constantly was to ward off this! You can't go around like an animal avoiding the consequences of your actions. It just isn't fair that these kids had to suffer because you wanted revenge on some idiot."

"You shouldn't have let him in."

She threw him a look charged with hatred. She suddenly stood straighter, and her voice took on a lower tone. "You're right, of course. I shouldn't have let him in, and I'll have to live with that. Now you can go. This is it, Mart, for good."

"Don't mix up *us* in this, Ella—"

"There is no *us*, Mart. No Mart and Ella, hand in hand. Haven't you noticed? I'm fed up with that and don't want it. And don't want you."

So here it was, at last. Ella was giving him the Loud Good-bye, and he knew that she meant it. He'd seen it coming for a long time, though he hadn't wanted to admit it. So why was he hammering on about this? With Ella lost to him, and Sorb just a dizzy shade of his former self, why was the distinct tang of love flooding even more generously toward them both?

238

What was the reason behind the unchartable tide? He didn't know, didn't care, didn't have time to ask questions—they had to get out first, and understand themselves later.

"The point isn't *us*," he said again. "Or, I'll say, it *is* us. All of us. We're going to get out—"

"You're going to get out," she snapped, "right now. I have work to do."

"Oh, cash it in, Ella, with the dramatics, will you?" He felt his own blood start to move around. "First things first. It's not child rape that happened here, for God's sake. I'm sorry about it, but the fruits are worth picking. Listen to me, we're not all that far from a real Groundhog Day."

"You're not going anywhere when the j-guards catch up with you." She was down on her knees, mopping the brows of the children and trying to move them into a line so they'd be easier to tend. Tachi seemed semiconscious, and was crying big tears, soundlessly. The others were knocked out. "Go on, leave. I mean it."

He knelt down on the other side of Belinda Ackerholm. Wiped a touch of spittle from the corner of her mouth. "I'm not kidding around, Ella. It started as a joke, but it isn't anymore. We're close to having the goods that will open the hatch."

"I don't care."

"Did you hear what I just said?"

"I did and I said I don't care. So go open the hatch. Let nine thousand tons of gravel and rubble come pouring in and kill us all. I don't care. I might even get

239

on the diatone myself and get the j-guards here to get you. You can't go marching around like a prince and no regard—"

"Will you *please* make some attempt to bridle yourself? And listen to me? I'm not talking about a pot dream. I mean really, truly, *out*. It hangs on Sorb getting the u-tool and my being able to figure out some missing digits in the passage code. It's within reach. It's spectacular."

"Do you really think, Mart," she rolled back on her heels, "do you really imagine you can break out of here? You alone of all these people? After all these years? Who do you think you are? The first thing that'll happen is an alarm'll go off. Or your neck will snap when the hatch opens and you're crushed by a flood of tonnage. Why do you think no one has left before? This isn't a space bus you can get off when you like. What's happened to that fancy high-powered brain of yours?"

"Listen—"

"Or you will get out. Let's say you do. The Elders will make up some story and say you're in the chiller, and nobody will be the wiser, and life here will go on for all these kids just like before."

"I'm not going to die here," he said. "I think Sorb is onto something. I think he knows that the tunnel is clear. I think it's always been clear. I think we never got out of here because we lost all connections with the world outside and we're afraid we'll die of radiation, or worse, loneliness and broken hearts. And we've been dousing ourselves with larmer—you know this!—and keeping our hopes moldy and diseased all this time. It's not a conspiracy by the Elders, I don't think. They're just as trapped and scared and dull as the rest of us. All I know is this— there's just one chance to get out, and the Elders are never going to attempt it."

"Now you're being dramatic."

"Well, so. So I am. Wouldn't you rather straighten up your spine under a broad sun, and see clouds, and see what's *happened* to the world, instead of being pushed around by Mon Conway and the gnatty little voices of everybody busybodying around? We were born under the sun and we deserve to die under it. Too much of eternity is going to be spent buried in the dust as it is."

"Makes sense to me," said Charles.

"Well what do you think?" said Mart. "What do you say, Mem Ella Mencken? Are you going to come with me?"

"You'll never make it to drylock, even, the way Mon Conway is after you."

"Well, if I do? And if Sorb comes through with the u-tool? You want to try?"

She sat back and looked at him. Her eyes were red and her eyelids swollen. Maybe she was remembering that funny love they had skirted around, never quite managing? Maybe she only had the little ones on her mind. He couldn't tell.

"Mart," she said at last, "I'll do this much. I'll take the kids out of drylock when you and Sorb try your escape. We'll come up to the hatch. Then we'll wait there. If you two get out, all well and good. I can't risk the lives of these kids in a dead world up there, it's not right. But we *can* go as far as the hatch, and stay there overnight. The parents of the kids will be frantic. The Elders won't possibly be able to cover it up. And whether you and Sorb get out or not, there'll be all these witnesses. Me and the little ones, and then all their families will know, too. I'll do that much for you—for all of us. I'll take everyone except the baby, Andrew. And Charles—the wheelchair will be too much to manage."

"Like hell it will," said Charles, wheeling closer.

29/ "Shoo, Fly, Don't Bother Me"

There was hardly time to make a plan. If the j-guards were truly after Mart in the way Mon Conway had hinted, then it would have to be a quick dash. Ella hurried back toward Jefferson with baby Andrew Afshar in her arms, there to wait for Sorb (because Mart couldn't be seen in public). She was reminded of all the 2-D films she'd seen in the past. It wasn't so much the racing, conniving, surviving she remembered well, but the film scores that accompanied the action. She imagined scores of violinists off to one side of her, sawing away in furious dissonance. Then the tympani lording it all over the melody. The discord, the rising of keys by eerie half steps, the sudden silences where a single breathy reed ventures forward into a new area of melody. . . .

It seemed she would never get there. But when she came into Jefferson, with her footsteps hard as hammers and her muscles aching in her calves, Sorb was sitting calmly, talking to Mem Dora. "Did you? Did you?" she said to him, and "Excuse me," then, to her.

"Did I?" said Sorb.

"Get it! The u-tool, Sorb!"

"Oh." He smiled, and patted his tunic, which she now saw was marvelously lumpy with instrument.

"Sorb!" She handed the baby to Mem Dora and then threw her arms around Sorb, almost losing her balance. "Oh, you did good work! Do they suspect?"

"Well, they must, soon, but now we've got to go."

Mem Dora said, "What's the big secret, you two?"

"We're leaving," said Sorb, before Ella could make a sign to stop him. "We're going. Now. Do you want to come?"

"Going where?"

"Out. Home."

"What? Mem Ella, what is this?"

Ella's voice was low and steady. "There isn't time to explain this all. Mart is in trouble for stealing tools and they're on his trail. But Mart thinks he can get the hatch open—"

"That's impossible—"

"—he thinks he can, listen to me, and Sorb says that the tunnel is clear. And I don't know myself, but I'm going partway with them, Mem Dora, and I'm bringing my children with me. Because if we make it to the hatch and stay out all night there, there's no way the Elders can cover up the fact that six little ones are missing. They could lie about the three of us, they could put us in the chiller like Garner Jones, but you know and I know that the one thing that would rile up

244

the colonists is if their small ones were missing. Little ones don't lie. It's a gamble, and I won't subject the baby to it, but I'm taking the others, and may all hell break loose whether Sorb and Mart get out or not. They can't ignore our attempt then, and maybe it'll spark some more action."

"Ella, that's irresponsible—that's not like you—"

"I don't care what you say. You have about ten seconds to make up your mind. You of all people know the power of a parent protecting a child. They're looking for Mart now; we'll have to sneak through the gallery in order to get to northpoint drylock. There's really no time to lose, as they say."

"You'll never make it," she said, "but I don't care. Try. You must go get Margaret, though. She'll be a good witness, too."

"What?"

"Go get Margaret. Take her with you."

"*You* go get her and come!"

"I can't come. I can't."

"We can't argue," said Ella, impassioned. "Why *not*, for God's sake?"

"If Sorb and Mart get out," said Mem Dora, "you know we'll all be out ourselves shortly. You're right: The Elders can't cover up your escape or lie about you if you've got the little ones with you. Get Margaret from Mon Draper's classroom. Bring her with you. Take care of her. I'm needed here. I'll make a loud fuss when she's gone tonight, I promise."

"Don't you want to say good-bye?"

"You're going to be late, you said so yourself, now

go!" Mem Dora then grabbed Ella and Sorb in a clumsy embrace that seemed to last forever, and that drew Ella and Sorb together in her arms, nearly face to face, although all eyes were downcast, and all hearts—or so Ella surmised—were heavy and light at the same time. "Godspeed, Sorb, and Mart too. And good luck, Ella! And don't forget Margaret!"

"What's one more?" said Ella. Mem Dora, who was behind them now, out of sight, was promising: "I'll lead the clamor to know where the children are, I swear! And I'll be in the gallery in half an hour, I'll cover your passage through there—don't worry!"

Sorb went loping toward the glass garden. His off-center grin was enough to give everything away. Ella found her breath coming in compact gasps, in and out—but there were alarming, dizzy hours between gasps, in which her system seemed to be working without the benefit of oxygen. Subsisting on persistence-of-vision-type hope, built from all the dreams, stories, memories, and Episodes in which people had attempted to do something daring, grand, or seditious, and had actually *managed* it.

The thought that success wasn't just a grape cluster hanging above Tantalus, but that the grapes *could* be snatched, hunger abated and thirst slaked, freedom grabbed hold of.

Buoyed up by the excess grandeur of Goringham's *Concerto for Two Pianos and Orchestra*, which played too loudly through her planning and fearing, she reached the classroom and knocked twice, remem-

246

bered she was a mem, and opened the door and walked in.

"Where's Mon Draper?" she demanded.

"Where's Sorb and Mart?" said a testy child named Boris Lachree. "Everybody's on the lookout. Off to their sweetheart again, huh? Feel left out, huh?"

"Watch your tongue," she snapped. "I asked you a question."

"Mon Draper's off walking the little ones to the toilet, Mem Ella," said another child. "He'll be back in a little while."

So Ella turned and left the room, and intercepted Mon Draper in the hall. "I've come from Jefferson Compound, and I need to take Margaret Prite with me immediately."

"Imperious tone in one so young," he said snidely.

"Not meant to offend," she said, "but the call's gone out for Margaret. There's some problem."

There was no diatone in the hall with which Mon Draper might verify her statement. "She's the last in, with her partner. I'll leave you to escort her if you'll drop her partner off at the classroom." With a sneer, no doubt to go checking with the Council at the first diatone.

The melody inside her ceased beating and whipping, and suddenly the back of her mind opened up into arches, and outside the arches spread an orchard, up a gently graded slope, and the smell of plum blossoms ran freely on the casual current of air. A sun generous as—as only suns can be, no metaphor can take the sun's place—that sun set down its heat in layers thin as pastry sheets, wave after wave of invisible drifts of goodly warmth. And around the gnarled trunks and crimped blossoms played the old sentimental processional music of Holst, the interior section of the "Jupiter" piece, the moving of stately beings toward peace. The music calmed her, the orchard opened up her small fears and ran them out in the sun to dry. She nodded to Mon Draper and said, "Go on ahead, I'll attend to Margaret and her partner."

So Mon Draper and the other children, whose bladders and bowels had already been relieved, turned away and walked decorously down the hall. Once they were gone, Ella, with her newfound solemnity, went into the toilet area and said lightly, "Margaret Prite? And partner? Come quickly. It's Mem Ella Mencken."

"Wait a minute, I'm not through," said Margaret, from a stall.

"Me, too," called the other voice.

"Hurry as fast as you can. It's important."

"I *can't* hurry," said Margaret. But she managed, coming out of the stall to be buttoned up again, because Ella was a friend and a buttoner at the same time.

"You too, hurry now!" said Ella.

Then the other came. It was Agnes Treasure. "We're in an awful hurry," said Ella. "Mon Draper's gone back to the classroom. Do you know the way back?"

"No."

"Don't you think you could find it this once?"

248

"No."

"I think you'll have to try. I have to take Margaret with me."

"We're partners. We're not supposed to split up."

"Toilet partners," said Margaret, giggling. "Also for letter writing and number writing."

"I can't go alone. I don't know the way," said Agnes tightly. She grabbed Margaret's hand and said, "We're *not supposed to split up.*"

"If you come with me," said Ella, "I don't want to hear another nasty word from you for the rest of your life. Do you understand me?"

"Of course I understand you. What do you think I am, stupid?"

"Now girls," said Ella, "we are going to *run.*"

An hour later they were on their way from the glass garden. The only provisions they had with them were the tools and a bunch of small ragged blankets to cover the children at night. The tools were hidden in the blankets, which were stuffed as carefully as possible in the rack underneath the seat of Charles's wheelchair.

It was that funny midpoint period in the afternoon, when the glass garden normally released its children to their compounds, so Ella had little fear of being seen escorting the children on the first part of the walk. But some assignments also let out at this hour, so Sorb and Mart had to keep hidden as much as possible to avoid passersby. The plan was to make it to the elevated walk around the gallery, and from there to cross out of the Centrex globe into the Utility Belt, and then through the northpoint drylock section of Pioneer. If Mon Draper had put in a report for Agnes Treasure, however, or if the j-guards and residents were really on the strict lookout for Mart, crossing the central gallery was going to be tricky. But it was the only path possible.

The melody inside Ella's head was contagious. Sorb and Mart were like clowns in their deft sidesteppings and fallings back, while Ella pushed the wheelchair, and Margaret and Agnes, hand in hand, led the sleepwalking kids. The mestrol check had enfeebled them only to the degree that docility had now replaced their usual midafternoon crankiness. Belinda and Glenda Ackerholm, Abe and Sam Mbulu, Tachi X'an walking alone, and Charles Trualt in the wheelchair.

They were taking a stroll, as once in a great while they did, only today the stroll would help foster a revolution, maybe.

Sorb, particularly, had a face like a golden mask. His hands kept reaching out, to touch Ella's shoulders, to link with Mart's hands, to pat Margaret on the top of her head, or to help Ella when the wheelchair encountered a difficult ridge in the iron floorpieces. "Don't be so happy, we haven't even made it through drylock yet," Ella whispered to him once, but he didn't hear her; he was beyond hearing anything.

Or so she thought, until they turned the corner into the dangerous passage that led to the most dangerous part of the route—the gallery. Then Sorb stopped short, hearing what she heard, a puzzled look coming

250

across him, as if for the first time in weeks sound had truly pierced him. Mart made a face. "The big escape!" he groaned. "You don't ask an entertainer to help direct this scene, for crying out loud!"

"Just keep moving," said Ella. "I guess that's the plan. Don't even look. Keep down below the level of the railing. We've lost our chance to take a last look. We've forfeited it. Just keep on."

"What is it?" said Margaret.

"Yuck, it's so *loud*," said Agnes.

Ella took a tighter hold on the molded plastic grips of the wheelchair. Her eyes stewed and stung. But no tears would fall—she was beyond allowing them to fall. The whole story had already been written, and this was only a postscript put in for effect. However, although she moved out into the passage, turned left and moved steadily and silently along, resolutely refusing to turn her head for even a fraction toward the sweet thunderstorm on the gallery floor below, she could see with the impatient reaching of her peripheral vision the small figure down there.

"Sometimes I feel like a motherless child."

Charles, who alone of the children had been spared the mestrol check because he'd been too much for Mon Conway to manage alone, crooked his neck a notch and tried to see over the edge of the rail. "Who's singing?" he said. "Sure is loud. Mem Ella?"

But Ella couldn't answer him. Her own inner music had left her, naturally, and the void was being

251

stamped with the sound of this colossal voice. The tempo was andante, the mood somber. Who in the past could have sung such a song as this, and for what terrible loneliness? Just about everyone, for just about everything, was what her rational mind was answering, but her other voice told her that Mem Dora wasn't singing for herself, or for the lost child Mazerius, or the current vanishing of Margaret, or the children Ella had in tow.

"Sometimes I feel like a motherless child."

She was singing for Ella.

Mart and Sorb were half crawling, half running on fours, like chimpanzees, and the children behind them kept steadily on, apparently unaware of the miracle that was occurring downstairs. Even Margaret didn't turn and run to the railing—thank God! How could Mem Dora have taken such a chance? But maybe she had just known that the midafternoon passersby would stand cold in their tracks, a respectful distance away, mesmerized. Mem Dora stood in the center of the gallery, turning around as she sang. Ella permitted herself a quick glance, and saw Mon Conway slumped on a bench with his face in his hands, looking—yes, thunderstruck.

"Sometimes"

—she held the note out, and with a deft twist at what should have been the very end of her breath, she sent the note rocketing up a sixth, and buffeting down

252

chromatically in a short whisper, clear as amber and as thick in tone—

"I feel like a motherless child,
A long, long, long way from home."

There was a silence then. They were almost around the edge, almost to the passage. Ella looked down. Slowly, applause, that dimly remembered habit from the past, began to flutter through the room, even as people's expressions turned grimmer, and their long-lived sourness toward Mem Dora took a stronger hold in the set of their teeth, the guardedness of their eyes. Ella saw old Mem Bettina in her colored kerchief, applauding with vigor, and Elder Saint Gabriel, too. And there was Mem Lotus, bobbing this way and that as she assessed the situation with Mem Waterhouse to one side of her and Mon Gorky to the other. Elder Fitchell blew her nose with a honk.

Then Ella caught Mon Conway's eyes. He had looked up, as if embarrassed at himself, and he and Ella were locked in a stare for a lightning-blue instant, until she flung her head aside, imagining with distress that the filmy skin of her corneas had been bruised and torn with that motion. For Mon Conway's glance, undeniably, had been one of penitence and longing, just for that instant. She could no more ignore that face than she could turn and look to check. This time it might be rage again. He might even now be putting two and two together when he saw that she wasn't stopping to hear Mem Dora sing at last.

He might be leaving his place on the bench and jostling through the crowd to get to Mon Micklersohn's side. She did not look back.

    "Shoo, fly, don't bother me,"

sang Mem Dora, and though the voice had changed in volume once they turned down the alleyway toward northpoint drylock, Ella could still hear the smile inflaming the tone of Mem Dora's voice.

    "Shoo, fly, don't bother me.
    Shoo, fly, don't bother me,
    for I belong to somebody."

    "I feel, I feel, I feel,"

sang Ella along with her,

    "I feel like the morning star."

30/ Groundhog Day

The children were behaving well. Getting them through drylock had been risky and fretful, but the children had been calm through it all. They had thrown their arms languorously around the necks of Mart and Sorb and Ella and had been carried through without so much as a whimper. Even Margaret and Agnes, heavier bundles, were shuttled through without protest or squirming. The gravity of the situation was becoming apparent to them.

It was only moving Charles in his wheelchair that posed a difficulty. That mechanism of drylock made up of scissoring alarm beams could be frozen, through Mart's tricks, but it couldn't be eliminated. So Mart and Sorb had to pass Charles through by hand to Ella, Agnes, and Margaret, and the chair had to be folded and in part dismantled before it would fit. They worked with patience and impatience side by side in their limbs, as if their muscles were twitching with massive electronic stimulants and chemical depressants simultaneously. But through it all, silence. Things got done.

"We're not supposed to be here," said Margaret once.

"Your mother knows you're here, and that's all right then," said Ella softly.

"Come, come," said Mart, pulling Sorb through drylock. "Now we seal it up again and on to the hatch."

Ella counted. Herself, Mart, Sorb. Agnes, Margaret. Charles, Glenda, Belinda, Tachi, Sam, and Abe. Eleven. Five males and six females. If Glenn Trenton had ever gotten better, he'd have been with them too. But as they made their way along the passage, and as she watched the little ones, she thought that there was no more on earth she could ask for. The little ones plodded along, with their poor eyes full in their still-shocked countenances, with their clothes all the wrong sizes, as usual. Sweaters buttoned so tightly you'd think circulation would be cut off entirely. Pants rolled up in comical cuffs. Shirts dragging, on a few of them, almost to the knees. The children held on to each other's hands not so much for company, Ella was guessing, but to keep themselves upright. And so, pair by pair of them, they tottered as if they were first learning to walk, or else old enough that they were about to forget how, for good.

"I don't remember," she said to Mart in a low voice, "is it a long walk to the hatch?"

"Well, how long could it be?" he said. She gave him

a look. "When you're as small as these ones are, it could be very long." He mumbled, "Sorry," and ran his hand absentmindedly on the back of her neck. But all her skin stood obediently in place, her scalp didn't shrivel nor her heart begin to pound. A time and place for everything, she thought, with a self-conscious smugness that was strangely consoling, under the circumstances.

The walk to the hatch, Lord have mercy, was agonizingly slow, with the tiny creaking gait of this parade of miniatures slowing the pace down to a crawl. Conscious as Sorb was of Ella's mothering—the great example of serenity, confidence, and concern—he tried to rein in his own impatience.

Ella had come forward in a different way than simply being granted mem status early could account for. As if in expectation of a natural and not an iron world into which they'd soon be born, Sorb's whooling undisciplined mind ran to images of fruit and flower. The curling away of drying husks revealing the perfection of an ear of corn, or the slow explosion of apple from the nestled clamp of sepals. Even, though he'd never so much as speak of it, that Botticelli Venus, tilting with beauty on the shell-white shell, with her eyes focused inward. The mantling of her from the one side with a robe of blossoms. The shower of her from the other side by a wind of blossoms. These, and her own nakedness, fully unimportant to her. Whose thoughts lingered in another atmosphere. Whose world was larger than anyone else could know.

257

His footsteps were in syncopation with the voice of the ghost. He now knew, at last, that the ghost was tired of the act of haunting him, and impatient to be allowed out of the task, out of the underground barrel, into the firm hand of the sky, where it could linger in polite anonymity among other heavenly residents, and wait for its proper job of haunting others *after* he was dead, and give up this silly self-haunting beforehand. The ghost spoke his name now in a steady and violent way, like a gate banging on a rusty hinge before the force of a gale wind. *Sorb, Sorb, Sorb, Sorb.* He'd almost learned to ignore it. In time, in time, the hatch will open and out through the tunnel you will lead me. Just give the children here a chance to rest in a circle, each one setting his or her head in the next one's lap, while Mart stands apart, ready to shred open the hatch with his bare hands, when we get there, and Ella sits too. She knows that sitting herself will help them relax, even for a brief couple of minutes. You can only flap and caw that word, my name and not yours—or not yet yours—you can't make us budge an instant earlier than Ella allows. But only wait, my teaser, my tempter, only wait until then.

Mart came over. "You're feeling okay?"

"Absolutely."

"It may be hard work getting through the tunnel. The grade was steep in spots, do you remember?"

"I don't remember. It'll be all right. The hatch will open and the sunlight will be splashing around the threshold, like bright autumn leaves blown in. Just wait and see, the sun will pull us out."

258

"Sorb. Don't get carried away. The sun won't be splashing on any threshold. There are at least four ninety-degree turns in that tunnel, I remember that clearly. We're likely to be in the pitch black the whole way."

Sorb, Sorb, Sorb, chanted the ghost.

"There's no turning back now," said Sorb.

"I hope you know what you've said to me," said Mart after a while. "If we open the hatch and are drowned in rubble, or if the hatch just won't open because of the pressure against it from the other side—well, this is the end of us for this show. There isn't any turning back."

"Be of good cheer," said Sorb.

"Cut the Dickens chatter," said Mart, but he couldn't help smiling.

"We'll be out. I have it on the highest authority." He felt himself looking so owlishly at Mart that his ghost grew jealous and jabbed him even more forcefully with his own name. *Sorb, Sorb, Sorb.* "All right, all right! Ella, can we get on with it now?"

"I guess so," said Ella. "Pumpkins, up and at it now. Stretch to the sky, that's it."

"The sky, the sky," yawned Belinda, "big deal."

"They're coming to. Thanks be," said Ella. "Although we have the worst ahead of us, for sure."

The hatch was before them at last. Mart felt as if someone had taken the brex-wrench and increased the tension in his spine, so that all those separate vertebrae were more intimately scraping against each other, and the vital fluid brought to a boil and steaming in his medulla oblongata. Underneath his hair at the nape of his neck he was perspiring heavily. He had the tools, he had most of the passage code. Working out the missing digits, and the proper sequence of the disengagement moves, would be a long process.

Mart had Ella sit the children down a good distance away, and then told them all it was going to be a matter of time. Just before it opened, Ella and the kids would retreat into an antechamber, which could be shut off with solid doors, to be sure to keep them from exposure to any contaminated air.

Mart was jittery. Neither he nor Sorb could predict what the state of the surface of the earth would be once they found it again. Perhaps the grandest of their desperate dreams would come true, and the world would be intact as they had known it in their childhoods. Or at least intact beyond the range of an A-Day attack. Perhaps there would still be urbs standing, and civilized voices still speaking harmoniously to each other through defense screens in banks, shops, training centers, and entertainment malls.

Or perhaps the world would be rubble, charred as a bone pulled from a campfire, and chewed as by a hunger-mad dog. Maybe the radiation pall would burn out their lungs within hours of emergence into the atmosphere. Maybe they would huddle in icy winds or scalding rains, and fall from exposure before they reached a single settlement. It was far too wide a choice of fates, and he cursed himself for permitting even a brief overview of them. Far better he should be surveying the missing slots of the passage code, and trying that out; a much more manageable prospectus, for him, obedient numbers in a machine somewhat subservient to him.

"Give the man room to work," Sorb muttered beside him. "Back off."

"Back off yourself, creep," he said affectionately.

"I am back. I'm just—"

"You're just a bit loco. Let's see, try a 3–0–3–mesh-2." No good. Same prefix, mesh-3. No. And on, and on, till mesh-8 made a different sound in the circuits, and he had hit the first jackpot.

"I'm not loco," said Sorb.

"You're just," panted Mart, punching in the next known stretch of code, "a bit *strange*. You remember that song, 'Lonely with the Paradise Look in Your Eye'? Get Ella to sing it."

"I will not," called Ella.

"It's a misnomer, if you don't mind," said Sorb.

"Don't take it personally, I'm very *fond* of weirdos," said Mart. "Ah ha! Ah ha! Chickadees, this is as easy as pie. Round two. We'll hit Fort Knox for our next big job. Let me just try to get the numbers—8–4–8–8–tork times 3, mesh, and . . . and . . . we'll try a 1, no go, try a 2, no go, try a 3." On up to nine, and none of them went. "Snag. Double snag."

"Mart," said Ella.

"Humblest, humblest, my heart it will a-crumblest. Sorry if my language offends." He was almost singing. If it wasn't a digit it was a function, which was a bit trickier, but his brain was nearly whistling like a steam kettle, and he ruled out mesh and tork intuitively, settling on the possibilities of kempte, orror, and vena-set. Vena-set was a most elaborate and difficult function for the apparatus to handle, and one that worked within a time limit which self-destroyed if the proper concluding keys weren't punched in on time. So he said, "Quiet, friends, this is the darkest hour. I'll be working like a beaver."

"A beaver," said Margaret from afar. "Is that the husband of a bee?"

"Shh," said Ella. "Come closer."

"No."

"Shut up or I'll shut you up," Mart snapped, more nastily than he felt; but this was important.

"Make her!" answered Agnes, across whose mouth he could hear a hand being slapped.

So: vena-set. Go. The digits flashed in a momentary conjunction, and then rearranged themselves, and then a third time, and the screen went blank. His mind flung itself into the abyss of all numbers and found a wrestlehold, no, a stranglehold onto the orotactical grid suggested by the three sets of numbers. He scrambled down the grid like a spider, aiming at each one of the three areas nearly simultaneously, assessing the median ranges, punching in guesses, correcting, correcting, correcting, tightening the web into a prison for the key number, and now it was trapped, and more and more possibilities were being whittled away, and in its naked cowering shame—7–0–7–4–anamesh—4. Punch.

He sat back on his heels, his breath caught under

262

his tongue and squirming like a small snake trying to release itself—

The screen darkened. His heels went backward onto the floor. "Oh, I can't—" and then the digits reasserted themselves again, and his breath came out with a little hiss.

"We lost it!" said Sorb faintly.

"We are *very nearly there*," said Mart. "I think that was the big break." His stomach was now writhing and his bowels felt explosive. "I think I'm going to be sick, can you believe it?"

"Stop and be sick," said Ella calmly, "and then keep going."

"No time. I have to keep going now." He vented an embarrassing trumpet blast of foul smell, felt soiled as an infant, and punched in the next part of the passage code.

She must have been dozing. There had been a racket in the tunnel, and Mon Conway had been leading a squad, but in the ambiguous climate of her dream was he coming to rescue them from throwing themselves overboard into the world, or was he coming to shoot them before they were able to do it? Why did he have his hand on the portable diatone, and his mouth curved to speak, and why did he look so painfully angry and sorry and, in that most perverse way, sweet?

And how could it be that she had had a dream? A real dream? Was she becoming larmer free, unsedated?

There was the warmth of small bodies against hers, as if she were a Beauty dressed in animal skins, but these animals still had their little hearts, and timid thin feltings of hair on their crowns, and hands that nestled quite unreservedly in near her warmer recesses and folds. She sat up and shook her head, and nearly asked for Mon Conway, but caught herself.

Beyond, in the spotlight, she saw Mart crouched in a tense position, half kneeling, half standing, and Sorb was beside him with his hands on his shoulders as if holding him there in that attitude of near reverence. The brex-wrench, in two broken pieces, was flung aside, and the u-tool hung foolishly from some joint to the left of the hatch. A strange noise was pounding in the air, and Charles Trualt was trying to comfort Glenda, who was crying. She sprang up and the coverlet of children followed her, clutching at her skirt.

"Mart!" she cried. "Not yet! Let us get back!"

She whirled around. The doors to the antechamber had suddenly clanged shut of their own malicious accord, some sly defense mechanism they hadn't guessed at. That was what had woken her. She rushed at them but they were, of course, locked: a rigid defense against possible invaders from outside. They were trapped in a chamber the size of the glass garden, between the doors and the hatch. They were like mice caught in a grain thresher.

She turned again and stared at the hatch. It was rotating slowly, left to right, and, as she stared, she saw that its perimeter, a separate circle of interlocking ferrule-ground units, was rotating in the contrary direction.

"Here it is," said Mart. "Sorry, Ella, I didn't foresee that door locking us out."

"You *didn't foresee it?!* With all your fancy tinkerings—"

"I said I'm sorry." His voice sounded oddly normal, though his face showed a storm of pain against bone white. His lips were pressed tightly, all the fleshy parts of them turned inside his own mouth. She couldn't see Sorb's face, but Margaret had run up to him now and flung her arms around his waist.

Then the hatch began to lift, from the bottom to the top, like a curtain rising in an old-fashioned theater. "Stand away, you!" she yelled. A thin tongue of some grainy material, like millet or powdered rice, inserted itself into the vestibule as the hatch moved up, and she shuddered at the awful sensuousness of it. "Back!" she barked. The tongue became a lip, a slice of curve pouring out onto the iron floorpiece. It had a shape like half a hill, and grew in proportion to the height of the rising hatch. Sifted through with pebbles, she saw, and tiny awful things like bits of root. It didn't crash explosively, but gently ran. How did it run? She searched her memories and recalled the image at last: It ran smoothly and inexorably, like sand through an hourglass.

We will die of germs, nothing more brutal than that, she thought coldly. Not even government-sponsored germs. Just the plain old kind our bodies have forgotten about.

265

The hatch had reached its limit, and locked into an open position. The sand and gravel had flooded perhaps twenty feet into the room. The hatchway was, top to bottom and side to side, a mouth disgorging a dirty beige vomit, and there wasn't room for a baby to crawl through.

"Well, here we are," said Mart.

There was a long silence as they stared. Abe Mbulu finally said, "Well, *now* what we gonna do?"

Sorb was pale as a corpse. His hands lifted off Mart's shoulders and were suspended in midair now, and Margaret had pulled away.

"The highest authority?" said Mart. "You, oh you—"

Sorb didn't answer, didn't flinch. He walked forward and kicked off his shoes, and his socks, and toed the edge of the mound with flexing motions. He seemed to be trying to speak. Ella felt nothing for him now, and she didn't hate herself for it. She looked at him and felt she was looking at a broken idea, that would be tossed out and forgotten for the rest of eternity, starting now.

She didn't care. Maybe the missing children would still prompt a revolution in Pioneer. But it would be out of her hands, now. She was divorced from Sorb and Mart now, and forever.

Sorb was undoing his belt, dropping his pants and kicking them off, removing his tunic. He took his tunic in his hands and ripped the sleeves off, and then ripped the front panel from the back. He stretched a sleeve between his legs, from his groin to the top of

266

his buttocks, and fastened it with his sash, like a loincloth. He said, "Mart, your sash," and Mart didn't move. So he took the sash himself from around Mart's waist, and arranged the front panel from his own tunic over his head. Like a turban? No, like a veil—covering his face and ears, ending at his meager collarbone and shoulder blades. He loosely tied Mart's sash around his neck.

"You'll choke," said Agnes Treasure. "Serves you right, too. You're not supposed to go with things around your neck like that."

Without a word, Sorb walked into the sand, which shifted treacherously into the vestibule. It clung to Sorb's hairy calves and thighs, creating a second skin that changed Sorb's coloring. The flood was both light and dense. Sorb flipped ripples aside with his hands and sand fine as dust sifted into the air, but the heavy weight of the hatch-wide apron of sand seemed barely to shift as he struggled forward. It wasn't drowning, was it, if you died in dirt? No, it was suffocating. He was up to his knees, his waist, and still not within three meters of the hatch itself. The sand filled his loincloth and rudely tugged the back part off, which then dragged like a peach-colored tail on the mound behind his pumping buttocks.

"Don't look," said Ella, turning away, not from modesty, but from a sense of horror far too ordinary to be comfortable. "Come on, you kids. Don't look."

31/ Abroad

Now, what was the difference between dreaming and waking?

Everything that had happened in the past seemed like a dream.

All there was now was the sound from the seashell. You could hear it if you put it up to your ear. It was a faraway hush. Strange how a hush could also be a noise. Music of the sea, someone had said once. Waves? The great tides tossing the bits of life up on shore?

Was that dreaming or waking, to hear those sounds? To think in your head of a sea, a vast sea to crawl out of or skate across, a sea to be delivered from?

The sound could as well be the pair of wings that Icarus used to cross the sea. The hiss of air against the fletched bevels. Or the sound of wax melting lightly in the sun, as Icarus loses his step in the sky, and the heartless sea mouths him up.

Or maybe the sound from the seashell is angel wings. The guardians who protect you in life and carry you, in death, across the sea. Is that the angel lowering itself? Is it here yet? Settling past and future in its wings, negating fear and hope, closing its wings over you?

Folding out the differences between waking and dreaming. . . .

Hovering, coming nearer, sounding like a seashell as it sinks to you. . . .

Sorb thought the angel had been caught in the spokes above them, been stayed. He thought the angel was there even though invisible. He thought of "Hark, the Herald Angels Sing." The herald angel sings in disgruntled surprise at having been caught in midair, under the pressing, mysterious, dove-sweet pressure of clouds.

The spokes were black and of a thousand different widths and lengths, and they jutted crazily from a central, lopsided column, this way and that, in every direction under the sun. Well, there was no sun. Maybe it was gone for good. But Ella had said, in a voice that seemed like a pair of lips against each of his ears, "No, I think this is just nighttime."

"What is it?" whispered Margaret. Her voice— every voice—was like two lips pressed into his head from two different directions—had something happened to the air? Or had voices always sounded this perfect? He couldn't remember.

"You should sing," he said to Ella. "Sing for us now."

"How can I sing," said Ella, "when we have food to worry about for these little ones? First Mart figures out the air at the hatch might be filling up with poison fumes—then there's no choice but to follow you—now here we are with our lives at risk—how can I sing?"

"How can you not?" said Sorb.

"What is it?" said Margaret again.

There were no stars. He was glad. He was glad there was a ceiling of soft cloud. The small ones, who'd never seen a sky, might have been too frightened, and fear they would go drifting off into the endlessness. As it was, the lot of them had their thumbs in their mouths, except Charles, who was cramped in Sorb's own arms—they'd had to leave the wheelchair behind.

"What *is* it?" whispered Margaret, a third time.

A wind sprang up. The exhausted children shrieked. Mart came forward and stood behind Sorb and said, "You'll be cold, you." He put his arms around Sorb and around the bundle of Charles.

"Tell them," whispered Ella, smiling in the dark.

"You tell them," he said. He was afraid he might be wrong.

"All right," said Ella. She looked up. There were tiny pellets fixed with meticulous care at the tip of every one of the thousand spokes. Ella said, "It's a tree."

There was a silence filled with wind and the night light, which came from no heavenly bodies, no torpa lamps. Perhaps it came from the disgruntled angel,

270

who must be standing among the branches, fixing itself. Take my ghost with you on your way back, said Sorb. I don't need it until I'm dead.

"It's not a tree," scoffed Agnes Treasure. "I know what it is."

"What?" said Ella.

"It's a mulberry bush."

It loomed above them, taller than the height of the gallery, spectacularly noisy with creakings and jostlings. The angel was preparing to be aloft again. The smell was impossible glory.

"You must be right," whispered Ella.

It touched itself, branch to branch, bud to twig, rustling like fragile live joyous bones. It was a bare skeleton about to grow its skin. In the distance, over the edge of the colony entrance from which they'd finally emerged, a long complement of its family stood, twitching their limbs in approval. Somewhere beyond was a lift of hill, a smudge of brush, a twist of pines.

The world still had distance, a horizon. It hurt their eyes to look.

"Well," said Sorb, taking the situation in hand as responsibly as he could, given the difficulty of behaving sensibly in the face of a miracle, "sing, Ella, you have to."

"All right," she whispered. "But what?"

"Sing the mulberry bush song," said Agnes Treasure in exasperation. "What else?"

Ella cradled little Abe up nearer her neck and took hold of Margaret's hand. Margaret knew what was to be done. She fed her hand into the grasp of Tachi, who linked with Glenda, and so on, Belinda, Sam, Agnes, Mart, and finally Sorb, with Charles almost asleep in his aching arms.

"Here we go 'round the mulberry bush,"

she started, and made a little step along the ground, and some more, and they all followed, their voices painting a sound in the air like a host of small flames.

"The mulberry bush, the mulberry bush,
Here we go 'round the mulberry bush,
So early in the morning."

PRIAPUS & THE POOL, IV
BY CONRAD AIKEN

This is the shape of the leaf, and this of the flower,
And this the pale bole of the tree
Which watches its bough in a pool of unwavering water
In a land we never shall see.

The thrush on the bough is silent, the dew falls softly,
In the evening is hardly a sound.
And the three beautiful pilgrims who come here together
Touch lightly the dust of the ground.

Touch it with feet that trouble the dust but as wings do,
Come shyly together, are still,
Like dancers, who wait in a pause of the music, for music
The exquisite silence to fill.

This is the thought of the first, and this of the second,
And this the grave thought of the third:
'Linger we thus for a moment, palely expectant,
And silence will end, and the bird

'Sing the pure phrase, sweet phrase, clear phrase in the twilight
To fill the blue bell of the world;
And we, who on music so leaflike have drifted together,
Leaflike apart shall be whirled

'Into what but the beauty of silence, silence forever?" . . .
. . . This is the shape of the tree,
And the flower, and the leaf, and the three pale beautiful pilgrims;
This is what you are to me.

About the Author

GREGORY MAGUIRE is the author of THE DREAM STEALER and other fantasies for children, and he is coeditor of INNOCENCE AND EXPERIENCE: ESSAYS AND CONVERSATIONS ON CHILDREN'S LITERATURE. He has served on the Caldecott Committee for the American Library Association, and reviews regularly for *The Kirkus Reviews* and *Five Owls*. He has taught at Simmons and Lesley colleges in Massachusetts and is an artist-in-residence at elementary and secondary schools.

An inveterate traveler—most recently to Greece, Italy, and Nicaragua—Gregory Maguire now makes his home in Jamaica Plain, Massachusetts.

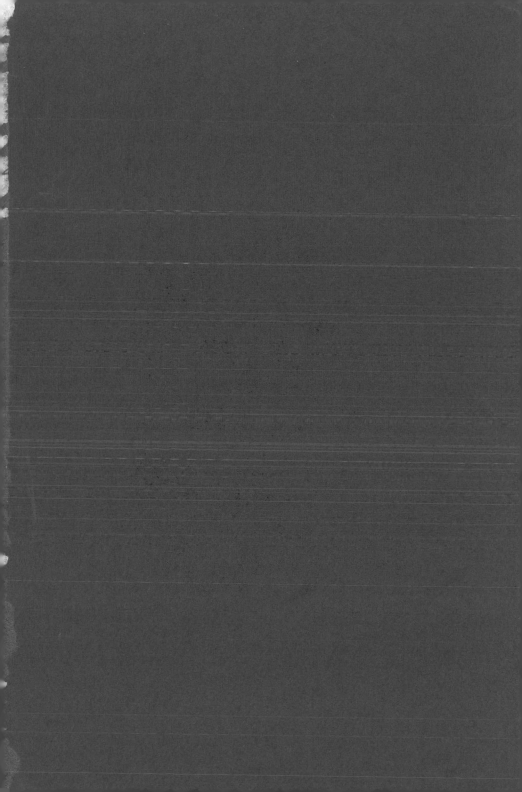